SEDUCING CECILIA

DIVINITY HEALERS

MICHELLE M. PILLOW

MICHELLE M. PILLOW® - MICHELLEPILLOW.COM

DIVINITY HEALERS BOOK TWO

Alternate Reality Romance, Part of the Divinity Universe

As things heat up, the clock is ticking, and the time for seduction is running out.

In a world obsessed with medical advancement, Dr. Gerard Fauchet longs for something more. When he's assigned as the liaison to a dignitary from a parallel universe, he never imagined she'd be so stunningly beautiful or so damned frustrating. One second she's kissing him, the next she's pretending nothing is between them.

The passion is scorching, everything he ever dreamed of having with a woman. He'll make her admit she wants him—or die trying.

Dr. Cecilia Markos is keenly aware that she's been shoved through a portal to an alternate reality for one reason—to bring home medical advancements for the betterment of her people. Unfortunately, she only has two months to learn a world's complete medical knowledge base. It's an impossible task made even more so by the distractingly handsome Gerard who she can't seem to keep her hands or her mind off of.

As the clash heats up between Gerard and Cecilia, the clock is ticking, and the time for seduction is running out.

In Asclepius there are only two classifications of people. Doctors and Not Doctors (Sans). They are the go-to plane for anything medical. In fact, they're so focused on health it's become a bit of an obsession. Plants are encased in glass to protect people from allergens. The air is pumped full of chemicals to keep it sterile.

This is a plane teeming with germ-a-phobes.

The Playful Prince
The Bound Prince
The Rogue Prince
The Pirate Prince

Captured by a Dragon-Shifter Series
Determined Prince
Rebellious Prince
Stranded with the Cajun
Hunted by the Dragon
Mischievous Prince
Headstrong Prince

Space Lords Series
His Frost Maiden
His Fire Maiden
His Metal Maiden
His Earth Maiden
His Woodland Maiden

AUTHOR UPDATES

To stay informed about when a new book in the series installments is released, sign up for updates:

michellepillow.com/author-updates

To My Awesome Readers.

Thank you for your emails, wall posts, tweets,

and for letting me do what I love by reading my books.

CITY OF ASCLEPIUS, COUNTRY OF CHIRON, DIMENSIONAL PLANE 187

DR. GERARD FAUCHET tried to hide the spark of jealousy he felt when he looked at his childhood friend, Dr. Sebastjan Walter. Sebastjan nodded politely as his guests moved through the receiving line to congratulate him on his new marriage. The son of the Medical Supreme, Sebastjan had lived an easy life. His family had money, position and political power. Medical Supreme Walter was easily the highest ranking official on the planet and he was in charge of allotting all of the planet's medical research funding. To a world obsessed with medical advancements, research funding was like air and bodily sustenance.

Gerard focused his attention on his friend. It wasn't Sebastjan's birthright or money or power or position that made the pang of jealousy filter over Gerard. It was Sebastjan's new wife—Ariella. A true, exotic beauty, Ariella came from an alternate dimension of reality. Ever since Gerard heard about inter-dimensional plane travel, he'd become obsessed thinking about it. He'd never really wanted to be a doctor. It was just what everyone on his plane was expected to become. He'd much rather spend his days reading and learning about culture and social history, than studying the readily available medical books that filled every home and office.

Like most nice homes in Asclepius, the front room of Supreme Walter's mansion was excessively sterile, each surface hard and unwelcoming but for a few engraved curls and wisps decorating the marble borders on metal walls. However, the Medical Supreme did have a vast array of items collected from other parallel universes. Gerard found himself staring at them, wondering about those other worlds. What kinds of places were they to dedicate so much time to books that told unreal stories, and to creating things of elegance and beauty for the mere sake of elegance and beauty?

When he looked at Ariella, he thought of all the things she knew—non-medical things, small facts that would mean nothing to her but would provide endless fascination for him. The women on his plane talked like doctors, thought like doctors, were mostly doctors. Not Ariella. She was a Sans, a non-doctor. Sans Ariella. And the very idea of her captivated him.

"Dr. Fauchet, how good of you to come," Sebastjan said.

"How could I not?" Gerard answered his friend. The loneliness that welled within him as he looked at Ariella became almost unbearable, so he hid it behind a playful smile and flirtatious wink.

"Couldn't miss my reception?" Sebastjan asked, skeptical.

"I couldn't miss the Medical Supreme's summons," Gerard corrected. "You didn't think everyone was here to see you, did you?"

Ariella gave a short burst of laughter at the insolent joke.

Gerard winked at her but continued talking to Sebastjan. "Apparently, I am to host two off-plane dignitaries coming here to learn our secrets. However," he turned his full attention to Ariella, "while I am here..."

He wasn't a fool. All the thoughts running through his head would never come to fruition. Though he found her very pretty, he didn't know her, not really. He simply liked the idea of her. He would leave the mansion and perhaps only cross paths with Ariella a handful more times in his life. Her tiny secrets would remain hers as she lived out her days as a doctor's wife.

"Sans Ariella," Sebastjan introduced, "my childhood playmate and local lawbreaker—"

"That is distinguished gentleman and dignitary host," Gerard corrected.

"Dr. Gerard Fauchet," Sebastjan finished.

"A great pleasure," Gerard said, playfully studying Ariella's face. "And it was only one tiny law fourteen years ago. There was a medication mishap, it was hot and it was only the male chairmen who complained about my nakedness. I swear I am a reformed man."

Sebastjan cleared his throat.

Gerard laughed, not showing a single second of remorse at having been caught flirting with the new bride. Leaning in to Ariella, he whispered, "An even greater pleasure to see you've managed to make Sebastjan jealous over you."

Ariella blushed. Sebastjan frowned at them. Gerard bowed his head and moved on.

"What? No present?" Sebastjan grumbled after him. Gerard laughed, but didn't turn back around.

NEW ORDER SOCIETY, DIMENSIONAL PLANE 303

Dr. Cecilia Markos stared at her foot, absently following the lines of her citizen number with her eyes. "One. Zero. Eight. Seven. Five." She didn't need to read it to know it. The tight, neat script had been inked into her flesh the day she was born. It concealed the newer implants the government had instated as an enhancement to the anti-chaos movement. She still remembered the day, as a child, she had watched the government trucks pull into her school armed with brightly colored animal costumes and silly songs. The characters danced and sang as the coded implants were injected beneath every child's number.

One. Zero. Eight. Seven. Five.

Those numbers were everything—her money

access, her workout logs, her doctor credentials, her purchasing rations, her identification. Everyone living in New Order Society had a designation. It was the only way a society could thrive. There had to be order to avoid chaos. Citizens needed to be monitored and watched. Control needed to be maintained.

Cecilia knew this, agreed with it fundamentally. Yet, despite her political beliefs, at moments like this when she was alone and unmonitored she couldn't help but wonder what chaos would be like. She didn't want wars or anarchy in the streets. That would be insane. But what about a night of passion that didn't include consent forms and planning? She knew it was wrong and she could *never* tell anyone her most secret thoughts, but when she closed her eyes she imagined spontaneity.

Just thinking about it made her heart race. What would it be like to break free? To kiss a man without waiting for an exchanging of permission? To feel passion, true chaotic passion that didn't make sense. It was something she could never act on. If she did, if the man she kissed complained or anyone found out, she would be fired. Her life would be over and she would spend the rest of her days in disgrace...if not jail.

Living in such a controlled world, it seemed strange then that she would be going to a place where those numbers on her foot meant nothing. A tiny shiver of fear washed over her. A few months ago, she'd never dreamed that visiting an alternate universe was possible. Now, she was to be one of two women going to a new world—another plane of existence, another reality, their world but not their world. Excitement mingled with fear, but she didn't allow herself to fantasize about the kind of men and sex laws this new reality would have. It wouldn't matter. On her plane or any other, she would be expected to exude anti-chaos values. She represented her people to the rest of the known universes.

An entity called Divinity Corporation had mastered the science of inter-dimensional travel and, two years ago, they had made contact with Cecilia's plane. Already a few of her people had gone through the portal gates to new dimensions. When Politician Shinclus first approached her, she'd thought he needed medical attention. The existence of the portals wasn't common knowledge amongst her people. But she'd since seen it for herself. She watched as people appeared out of nothing, carrying strange objects traded from other realms.

A few short months and so much had changed.

All the waiting and planning, reading and studying, worrying and pretending not to worry, had all led to this day. Today, she would be traveling to an alternate reality.

The New Order Society plane was only one of four-hundred-thirty-six mapped dimensions used by Divinity—each as different as the last. Some had vampires and werewolves, some had faeries and gnomes, and some had humanoids so alien her dimension's species were hardly compatible. Many of them, like hers, had never even heard of dimensional travel or portals until Divinity arrived. Some societies were obsessive to the point of compulsion and some so brutal they enjoyed watching gladiators fight to the death. One thing many of them seemed to have in common was chaos. Utter, uncontrolled chaos. New Order Society thrived on anti-chaos—no unconformity, no inappropriate behaviors, and absolutely no crime. Well, minimal crimes anyway. There was definitely no tolerance for criminal activity.

Looking at an alternate reality was supposed to be like seeing your world had history unraveled differently. There were many similarities. Languages were comparable. Some people had the same appearance, but were not the same people. Certain events like natural disasters could be shared. People were human-like in appearance and functions, though she had been told of a race of people that didn't have toenails.

Cecilia wiggled her toes, wondering what they'd look like without nails. Then, sighing, she stood and reached for her best one-piece suit. Red material belled around the legs and led up to tightly-fitted hips and a looser bodice. The sleeves were long, falling past her hands. She brushed her hair back from her face, trying not to think about the fashionable crimson red streak she'd been forced to get rid of. Apparently, this medical plane she was going to didn't have the same fashions. In New Order Society everyone sported a bright streak of color in their hair. Just because they were orderly didn't mean they couldn't be fun too. Well, that and the streak proved the wearer had been to their mandatory grooming appointment by the lack of a line of demarcation where the new growth came in.

Taking a deep breath, Cecilia pulled on her boots, whispering, "It's only for a couple of months. It will be fine. It's only two months. I'll be able to make it back. Everyone else has made it back home."

Despite her words, she wasn't so sure.

A COUPLE of months looked like an eternity when staring into a Divinity portal. A pyramid roof set atop four square columns which framed a platform. Cecilia had memorized the literature on the device. The columns were constructed of a dense material which created its own gravitational field and drew objects to it. They hid a complex configuration of liquid crystals, electrical currents, mirrors and vacuums. It was held in check by the wavelength of a specific blue light, which kept the portal inactive. Should the light change, a dimensional shift would occur, taking whoever stood on the platform to a new parallel universe.

Cecilia didn't move. All the facts in the world

were doing little to calm the increasingly fast beat of her heart.

"You know, Politician Shinclus told me that people sometimes get rematerialized into solid objects when going through these things," Linnea Nel, Cecilia's new assistant said.

Cecilia glanced at the woman. Such occurrences had been reported in the early day of portal travel. Now Divinity sent out microscopic probes first. Even so, it wasn't exactly what she wanted to think about at the moment.

Linnea hugged a stack of papers to her chest a little too tightly. Cecilia had only known the woman for a few weeks, but already she didn't care for her. Before this assignment, Linnea had been in and out of trouble with the authorities. Plus, she was a non-conformist. For some reason, the New Order Society implants didn't work inside Linnea's body. They believed it had to do with her natural magnetism and electrical current—not that she shot lightning out of her fingertips or anything absurd, just that for some reason computers didn't always work around her. Without an implant, Linnea was like a ghost, uncontrollable, untraceable, chaos waiting to happen. Sure, she had the identifying tattoo, but one had to look at her foot to see it.

"He was just trying to scare you," Cecilia answered, refusing to let any fear show. She was already nervous enough about traveling through the portal. "Politician Shinclus is known for his bad humor. It is true accidents happened in the past, but that is why they send out the probes first. Besides, where we are going is a known destination and an opposite portal will receive us on the other side. Everyone there works for the central hospital government in some capacity. It should be like going to a giant hospital." She turned to study Linnea. The blue light from the portal reflected in the woman's eyes, giving them an eerie glow. The woman's black hair was shorter with a streak of dark purple to match the purplish grey of her eyes. Her bodice was tight, less conservative in design. A thick, black belt wrapped her ribs, dark purple over black material. "Weren't you supposed to change your hair?"

"I didn't make it to my appointment. Something else came up." Linnea arched a brow. "I don't really think it matters all that much. I'm sure they'll make allowances for our alien customs."

"The plane we're traveling to does not know of our fashion customs. We might unintentionally insult them. Did you read the recommendations report put together by the Committee for Interplane Diplomacy?"

"I was going to," Linnea drawled, "but I was in the middle of a different book at the time. I wanted to finish it before we left."

Cecilia closed her eyes, too weary to argue at the moment. She had too much on her mind. She had to represent her entire planet in what could possibly be the most important trade agreement ever negotiated in the history of their society. Who knew what kind of medical advancements this plane would be able to show them? What if they could advance their medical technology by years, hundreds of years, thousands of years? She would need to focus and learn and observe. Glancing at Linnea, she frowned. And by all evidence she would be busy apologizing for the controversial woman they were sending with her. How Linnea managed to get sent on such an important mission was beyond Cecilia's reasoning.

Linnea smirked as if she hadn't a care. Workers began filing out of the room, leaving them alone with the portal. Cecilia frowned, saying, "It's too late to do anything about your hair now. We will be leaving soon."

Without waiting for Linnea to speak, Cecilia moved toward the platform. Her luggage had already been sent ahead. It had been strange to see it disappear into seemingly nothingness. A low, steady hum sounded moments before a voice could be heard overhead, ordering, "Dr. Markos, Citizen Nel, please report to the platform."

Cecilia concentrated on keeping her legs steady and her chin up. She was in charge. This job, this mission, would open so many doors for her career. If she worked really hard and kept the delinquent at her side in line, she could do great things. Such an opportunity for advancement would not show itself again.

Once on the platform, she turned her attention toward the source of the light beam. It hurt her eyes, but she knew behind it would be the control booth's window where technicians would be manning the controls and the politicians in charge of this secret project would be looking down at them.

"Prepare for portal travel," the controller announced.

"See you on the other side, Doc," Linnea said softly.

The light began to change color, shifting into a pale green. Cecilia's flesh tingled, tightening as if being pulled away from the bone. She braced herself, knowing that portal travel was reported to hurt.

Nerves bunched in her stomach and she held her breath. The humming grew louder. She closed her eyes to the bright light.

Heat burned her flesh and she felt heavy, but she didn't move. Cecilia would have screamed, but she had no voice. Her body pulled apart at a molecular level. Then, as quickly as it started, it stopped. She fell to her knees, gasping for breath. Linnea collapsed on the floor next to her, coughing as she dropped her papers.

Cecilia took several deep breaths, not bothering to get up as she looked around. A sweet scent filled the air, subtle and not exactly unpleasant, but different. Blue light shone on them, not looking as bright as the one on their side of the portal. A loud alarm sounded, blaring over them.

"So loud!" Linnea said, her voice lifting as she covered her ears.

"Sterilization commencing," a male voice announced, louder than the alarm. When she looked, she didn't see anyone. "Please stand and move away from the platform."

Linnea gathered the papers and pushed to her feet. Reaching down, she pulled Cecilia up by her arm.

"Please stand and move away from the platform," the voice repeated, even louder.

"I think that's us," Linnea yelled over the alarm. Both women obeyed. Linnea didn't let go of her and Cecilia found that, for the moment, she was grateful to not be alone. The room was constructed of shiny metal—from the floors to the walls to the ceilings. A shield slid down from the ceiling, blocking the platform. They both turned, startled, watching it.

"Welcome, dignitaries from New Order Society, Dimensional Plane 303, to Central Hospital and Optimal Health Centre in the City of Asclepius, Country of Chiron, Dimensional Plane 187. We are now scanning you for foreign dimensional parasites and viruses. Please do not move until scanning is complete." A series of lights followed the male's orders, flashing over them. The alarms stopped, leaving her ears ringing. "Sterilization complete. Please state your clearance code."

"Dr. Cecilia Markos," she answered. "New Order Society dignitary."

"This is tedious," Linnea muttered. "I hope they don't all talk that loud."

"Voice recognition accepted. Please move to the orange door." The door was actually metallic gray with a series of numbers and letter written in orange across the front. It opened automatically.

"It's only for a couple of months," Cecilia said under her breath. She led the way through the door, forcing herself to be brave.

"Yeah," Linnea answered, "but two months of what?"

GERARD WALKED through the secured halls of the Central Hospital and Optimal Health Centre building toward the Divinity portal hidden within. Studying his electronic clipboard, he checked over the visitors' sterilization scans results before signing off on them to let the visiting doctors inside the main complex. This assignment was more like a child-watching mission, but he didn't care. He'd lied when he told Sebastjan he was summonsed to meet the dignitaries. The truth was he'd volunteered. How could he resist the opportunity to meet off-plane visitors?

The overhead alarm would continue to buzz until he signed his name. Doing so quickly, he relaxed as the buzzing stopped. He hurried through the metallic gray corridors of the hospital. It looked like an endless maze with only the orange lettering on the walls to give directions. Any unauthorized visitors would be lost.

"It's only for a couple of months."

Glancing up, he started to smile. The look faltered.

"Yeah, but two months of what?"

He glanced back down to the clipboard to gather his wits. His information didn't say anything about the doctors being pretty. The slightly shorter woman carried a stack of papers. Her shoulder-length, black hair was streaked with dark purple and matched the strange shade of her purplish-grey eyes. Gerard wondered if it was a genetic anomaly or common for her people. But then, as he studied the other woman, all thoughts stopped. She was tall and proud with just a hint of disdain and fear in her voice as she'd spoken.

It's only for a couple of months.

Clearly she didn't look forward to this assignment. Gerard found himself fascinated. Though, if he were completely honest with himself, he'd admit that his fascination also had to do with the fact that this off-world woman caused a sudden surge of hormones to run rampant through his body. He shifted his hips, glad that the standard-issue facility uniform, a long, blue coat with red trim, hid his growing erection.

Knowing he had to get his wits about him, and fast, he cleared his throat. "Welcome..." Gerard hesitated, suddenly unable to remember their names. The tall one looked directly at him. Her brunette hair was pulled away from her face, giving him a clear view of her blue eyes. Her clothes were a strange style, but that was to be expected considering her origins. "Welcome, doctors."

"I'm the doctor, Dr. Cecilia Markos," the object of his sudden attentions answered tersely. Her hard tone only served to pique his interest more. She motioned to the woman with the papers. "This is my assistant, Linnea Nel."

Linnea gave a rueful smile at the other woman's introduction.

"Welcome, Dr. Markos, Sans Nel," Gerard amended.

"Thank you," Linnea answered. Cecilia nodded once.

"I am Dr. Gerard Fauchet. I will be your guide while you're on our plane. Anything you need, all you have to do is ask." He motioned to the papers. "Would you like me to carry that for you?"

"No, I've got it." Linnea glanced at Cecilia and added wryly, "I am the assistant, after all."

"We don't work with parchment, but I can have one of the doctors scan your documents into a clipboard if you like." He lifted his electronic clipboard to indicate the device he was talking about. "In fact, I understand supplies are waiting for us at the assigned research facility."

"You mean," Cecilia glanced around. "We will not be working here? Near the portal?"

"Afraid we might keep you here against your will?" Gerard teased. Cecilia didn't appear to appreciate his humor. He let the playful smile fall from his lips. In a more businesslike manner he stated, "Please, follow me."

Cecilia tried to smile, but the more nervous she became, the harder it was for her to act pleasant. All around her was a parallel world. It was not lost on her how impossible it would be to just run home and pretend none of this ever happened. Now this stranger—someone who until recently she would have said was the figment of an overactive imagination—wanted to take her away from the portal? What was she doing here? Was she crazy to agree to this? No one from her world ever stayed away so long.

Dr. Gerard Fauchet made her nervous. She wasn't sure about the way he looked at her. It was almost too familiar, too friendly, too interested. And she wasn't sure about the way his attention made her feel. How could she maintain a sense of professionalism if the man in charge of showing her around stared at her like she was already naked and in his bed? This wasn't the first time a man in power tried to play that game, and like the others she would quickly put him in his place. Only here, he wouldn't need her to sign consent to be in his bed. Or did he? She wasn't sure what their laws were. They were civilized doctors. It was entirely possible plane 187 would require informed consent before Dr. Fauchet could act on his leering expressions.

Oh, but what if he didn't have to? What if he could do what he wanted, when he wanted, how he wanted? Her breathing deepened.

Concentrate, she thought, *anti-chaos, anti-chaos, anti-chaos...*

She took another deep breath, proud of herself for maintaining control.

So why, exactly, was she looking at his ass while he walked?

Cecilia's eyes darted up to his back. Next to her Linnea chuckled knowingly, or in a way Cecilia translated to be knowingly. She took a deep breath, almost choking on the sweet air freshener the hospital utilized.

"Doctor?" Gerard inquired at her cough. He looked at his clipboard and then at her.

Cecilia touched her chest lightly. "I am still adapting to the air."

He arched a brow and she found the expression slightly infuriating.

"It smells like we're walking near a confectionary," Linnea observed. "The air is very sweet."

"That is the air-filtering sterilizer," Gerard said. "The air is continuously tested for abnormalities and purified. You have nothing to fear here. We haven't had a serious illness for, well, some would argue for centuries now, depending on your particular definition of serious." He gestured absently toward the ceiling. "I am told that after a time you will become accustomed to the scent. We tried modifying the formula to be unscented, but it lost two-point-three percent potency."

"No illness for so long?" Cecilia questioned. She gave a meaningful look to Linnea. The woman's face was a blank mask. Then, realizing that maybe she expected too much of a reaction from a non-conformist semi-criminal, Cecilia turned her attention back to Gerard. She watched the shift of his shoulders beneath the lab coat. It was a subtle movement, but she found herself staring at the hypnotic play of muscles. "That is quite the accomplishment."

He glanced back at them. "Indeed."

Gerard led them through the hall, turning several times until Cecilia gave up trying to remember their path. Monitors on the wall showed their life signs as they passed, very similar to the scanners on her home plane. Only, instead of reporting a picture ID, it reported heartbeats and temperatures. Her heart was beating a little fast.

When he stopped, Gerard turned his attention to her. His voice was low as he observed, "Your lidec levels are elevated. Would you like me to alleviate your..." he paused, "*symptoms?*"

The way he said the word "symptoms", all low and warm, caused a sudden shock of pleasure to spread through her stomach. It radiated over her pussy and thighs. His eyes seemed to smolder with intent. Lidec? Symptoms? Did that mean her arousal? Was he propositioning her? Did the monitors reveal her interest in him?

"Ah, Dr. Fauchet." The abrupt sound cut into her thoughts and directed her attention to the older man coming down the hall. By the self-satisfied look on his face, she assumed him to be the man in charge.

"Dr. Markos, Sans Nel, may I present Medical Supreme Walter, his son Dr. Sebastjan Walter and Dr. Walter's wife, Sans Ariella."

"Doctor," the Medical Supreme acknowledged,

glancing only briefly at Linnea. He had a smooth, youthful look to him that contrasted the intelligence in his blue eyes. A foreshadowing of gray salted the black hair at his temples.

"Welcome," Dr. Walter said. Ariella nodded.

"And this is the hospital coordinator, Dr. Lu," Gerard finished. Dr. Lu stayed back behind the others and she didn't get a good look at him.

"Welcome to Asclepius," the Medical Supreme said. "We look forward to a mutual exchange of knowledge. I have chosen Dr. Fauchet to be your guide. He will remain at your side. Should you need anything, please speak directly to him or to Dr. Swift. I will be unable to attend you at the research facility. I am a very busy man, after all."

Cecilia began to answer, but the Medical Supreme cut her off.

"Here he is!" The Medical Supreme lifted his hand, motioning behind them. "May I present the esteemed Dr. Swift, Director of Central Hospital."

Dr. Swift nodded at the visitors. His gaze lingered on Linnea's hair a long moment but his expression gave nothing away.

"It is good to meet you, doctors," Cecilia said.

"Dr. Markos," Dr. Swift acknowledged. Behind him Sebastjan slipped away with his wife. The quiet

Dr. Lu soon followed. Cecilia thought their abrupt departure odd, but chose to ignore the obvious plane custom. "I've ordered your transport readied. Your belongings have already been loaded. Dr. Fauchet will show you where to go. I must attend to a few matters here but will join you later at the facility."

"Sans Nel has parchment to be transferred to a clipboard. Perhaps she should work here and arrive later with you when she is finished?" Gerard suggested.

Dr. Swift didn't spare Linnea a look as he nodded. "Very well. Sans Nel, follow me. I will show you where you can work."

"Where did my son...?" The Medical Supreme began to question, glancing around. Then, as a severe frown crossed his features, he said, "Excuse me. I have urgent business to attend to."

Before Cecilia fully realized the implications of what was happening around her, she found herself alone with Gerard. He smiled at her, a playful, almost achingly seductive look. There was an ease to his mannerisms that took her by surprise and didn't seem to fit with the others she'd just met.

"You're very pretty," Gerard said.

Cecilia opened her mouth to answer, but no sound readily came out.

"Are you with someone? Married? Taken? Do you have such customs on your plane?" he questioned.

"Ah, no, I'm not taken," Cecilia managed, not sure she should answer such a personal question but unable to think of anything else to say.

"Brilliant. I'm pleased to hear it." His smile didn't fade. And was it just her imagination, or was he leaning closer? The thoughts racing through her mind were anything but anti-chaotic.

Cecilia watched his lips move as he said something more but she didn't pay attention to the words that came out. The sweet smell or sanitized air was temporarily overwhelmed by the scent of his body. He smelled clean, fresh, not like the cleansers on her plane, but exotic and new. She found herself breathing deeply. With each inhale she shivered, and with each exhale she found her senses focused more fully upon him.

"Dr. Markos?" Gerard inquired, arching a brow. "Are you ready?"

"Ready?" she repeated. What had he been saying? For the life of her she didn't know. All she could think about was kissing him without permission. She cleared her throat and forced her eyes away from him. "Yes, yes, of course I am ready to leave."

Cecilia stepped slowly toward a box-shaped vehicle Gerard called a transport. It hovered over the ground outside the hospital. She took her time as she glanced over the carved stone landscape. The streets, sidewalks and buildings seemed connected by one smooth formation of rock. Statues rose up from the ground, their stiff lines and symmetrical features just as clean and orderly as their surroundings. Aside from the small plants encased in large glass boxes, they were the only visible pieces of life in the area.

The Central Hospital and Optimal Health Centre dominated the street like a centerpiece. Thick columns and oversized stone arches were mimicked by the smaller buildings. The outside architecture was nothing like the metal corridors within.

Gerard waited for her by the transport door. As she approached, he held out his hand, offering to help her up. Instead of steadying her when she placed a hand in his, he tugged her off balance. Cecilia fell toward him, landing against his chest. She blinked in surprise, gasping.

Warm lips found hers, pressing hard against her mouth. The kiss took her by surprise and she didn't pull away. Her knees weakened. Gerard held her to his chest. Firm muscles pressed into her softer breasts, making her very aware of the intimate moment. Heat filled her, radiating down her stomach and thighs.

Cecilia moaned softly, her lips moving of their own accord to accept his inappropriate embrace. In the back of her mind a thought whispered that this couldn't be happening, that it couldn't be real, that she wanted it too much and was delusional. He answered the movement of her mouth, deepening the kiss. His tongue slid into her mouth, gliding between her lips and teeth. She knew she should pull away, but part of her wanted to see what he'd do next.

Gerard's hands slid down to the small of her back and he turned, pressing her against the transport.

The solid feel against her back and the sudden thick arousal hitting her stomach caused her senses to come crashing back to reality. Gasping, she ripped her face away and pushed against his chest. His hand was lodged against her ass, frozen in a squeeze. For a moment, he didn't move as confused eyes stared into hers.

"Doctor!" she hissed in warning, keeping the word low. Drawing up her hand, she slapped his cheek, not so hard as to leave an imprint but enough to snap him to his senses. The action came from years of living in anti-chaos. It was how she was supposed to react to such a presumption. Had he done that on the city street back home, they would have both been arrested. He let go and she pushed harder, forcing him to stumble back. The ache of withdrawal hit her like a cold rush of air. She shivered, resisting the urge to rub her arms. "What do you...? It is not..." she hesitated. "I am unfamiliar with your plane's customs, but you are taking liberties I am not willing to give. In my reality we have certain customs that must be followed to avoid any chaos or confusion. I certainly did not sign a consent form for your advances before coming here."

Cecilia hoped her words sounded properly diplomatic, even if the tone did not. Gerard's expression lost its playfulness. Slightly under his breath, he mumbled, "I am unfamiliar with your plane's customs, but generally if a woman is not interested she does not kiss a man back."

GERARD STEPPED INTO THE TRANSPORT, not waiting for the visiting doctor to go first. He wasn't really angry at her so much as he was irritated with himself. He didn't know what came over him—grabbing and kissing the visiting dignitary like that in front of Central Hospital where anyone traveling by could see. It didn't matter that the streets were mostly vacant this time of day.

He'd wanted her from the first moment and his desires had only grown. When she took his hand, he'd just reacted—without reason or sense. He'd meant the kiss to be short, but she'd responded to him. Her lips had parted. Her body had pressed, so warm and soft and feminine. She smelled exotically sweet, like the celebratory desserts his grandmother used to sneak him before the full enforcement of medical contraband laws. She had wanted him, if only for the briefest of moments.

Cecilia was slower to enter, but she did, taking a seat across from him. She pointedly looked everywhere but at his face, pretending to study the inside of the transport as he pressed a button to activate it. The coordinates had already been entered. Since the address was typed into the transport's computer, the occupants were free to enjoy the ride—no driver needed. It only took a few seconds for the door to slide shut and for them to be on their way. The vehicle moved soundlessly, hovering above the ground as it sped along Asclepius's self-navigating streets.

"You might want to get comfortable for the journey," Gerard instructed, stretching out his legs and shutting his eyes.

"Do all your cities look like this one?" Cecilia asked. When he opened an eye he found her staring out of the window. "Everything seems very orderly and quiet."

"No. Not all cities."

"Is it true everyone here works for the central hospital government in some capacity? How do you feed everyone if you all work for the hospital?" She turned her attention to him. "Don't you need farmers? Laborers?"

"Biologists provide sustenance with enhanced

properties," he answered. "Agricultural doctors deal with plant production and nutrient compounds."

"What about the crime rate? It seems quiet here. Our streets are very busy at all hours, though crime is low due to the anti-chaos laws. Do you have a way of tracking your citizens? Is that a function of the wall monitors?"

"You have a lot of questions and there will be plenty of time to answer them all. Are you nervous?" Gerard didn't move. "Is that why you are speaking so fast?"

Light smoke began to filter into the transport. It would help them to sleep for the ride. Cecilia coughed, covering her mouth. His limbs felt heavy as the drug filled his lungs. Her wide eyes turned toward him and her mouth opened in panic but she slumped over on her seat. Darkness crept over his vision and he let sleep take him.

7

WAVES LAPPED AGAINST AN UNSEEN SHORE, creating a constant, tranquil rhythm. Cecilia yawned, stretching in her seat. For a moment, she blinked heavily, forgetting where she was. Nothing looked familiar. Bringing her hand to her mouth, she yawned again.

New plane. Work. Dr. Gerard Fauchet.

Her attention turned sharply to the man sleeping in the seat across from her. He appeared completely relaxed, breathing evenly. She looked out the transport windows, finding nothing but an expanse of wilderness on one side and ocean on the other. They weren't traveling very fast and the unit even halted a few times, rocking the occupants. She looked out the window toward a large expanse of forest. The thick trees were so dense she couldn't see deep into the forest. Wind stirred the purplish foliage littering the unmarred forest floor. There were no paths, only dense underbrush. On the other side, a beach led toward an ocean. The sand was perfectly rippled by nature, unmarked by human feet. They were away from civilization. The transport stopped moving. She held her breath, waiting.

"Dr. Fauchet?" she whispered, reaching for his knee when the transport didn't move. She shook him gently. "Dr. Fauchet? Can you wake up?" The transport turned in a circle. "I think something's wrong with this vehicle. We're, well, I don't know where we are but we're moving precariously."

The vehicle jerked suddenly, tossing her forward into his lap. She braced her weight with her hands, managing to stop her fall before their bodies pressed tightly together. His knee wedged between her thighs. She breathed deeply, studying his face. He didn't move. Her eyes moved to his mouth. He'd kissed her without permission. It was clear such things as filing consent forms weren't needed on this plane, not like in New Order Society. What if she kissed him? Exhilarated by the privacy of the transport, she leaned forward and brushed her lips against him for the briefest of seconds.

Cecilia slowly pulled back, almost frightened by what she'd done. She quickly untangled their limbs and sat on the seat next to him. She tapped his cheek lightly, waiting to see if he knew of the liberties she'd just taken. "Dr. Fauchet? Gerard?"

He didn't react.

Cecilia frowned and tapped him harder, worried something might really be wrong. Here she was acting on sexual instinct and he could have a medical issue. She felt for his pulse, holding his wrist as she pried open one of his eyes. The steady beat of his heart didn't change and the vacant stare didn't waver. She knew when someone was sedated. "Dr. Fauchet? Can you hear me?"

When he didn't move, she let her hand rest against his face. He didn't appear ill, just sleeping. The texture of his skin was stubbled lightly by beard growth. Her lips tingled and she wanted to kiss him again. His attraction to her had been clear, eloquently expressed in the pressure of his mouth and the tight push of his body. She remembered the outline of his arousal pressed against her stomach. Desire leapt up inside her, heating her belly and moistening her thighs. She wondered what he'd feel like against her, naked and strained.

This was not supposed to be happening. She was

on assignment, a dignitary for her people. Spontaneously sexing up the first doctor she saw wasn't very dignified. Yet, as she touched his cheek, she felt herself inching closer to him. She breathed deeply, noting the exotic scent of his flesh.

Cecilia closed her eyes, forcing control over her body. Sex was not the first thing she should be thinking about. She reached for her hair and pulled it loose, scratching nervously at her head. "You really need to wake up now."

Fingering a hairpin, she grabbed his hand and poked it with the tip in an effort to stimulate a response. He moaned softly, the first sign of consciousness since she'd awoken. Heartened by the reaction, she poked him again, harder.

"Ow." He jerked his hand from hers, blinking rapidly. "What are you doing?"

"There is something wrong. We're—" The transport jerked, starting up again.

Gerard pushed up from his seat, looking out the window. "We're only halfway there. Why did you rouse me? What are you doing awake?"

"I don't know. I woke up and the transport had stopped. We're in the middle of nowhere and I thought..." She looked helplessly at him. Now that he was awake the transport seemed really small. "I thought we were in trouble."

"Splendid," he drawled. "There isn't enough of the sleeping agent to put us back out. We'll be aware for the rest of the trip." He studied his hand, examining the dot of blood on his skin. Then, as if deciding he'd live after such a tiny wound, he stretched his arms over his head.

"You say that as if you've never been on a trip." She frowned. "How long is it until we get there? A day? Two?"

"I've been on several trips and have only been awake for a few of them." He suppressed a yawn. "As for this one, we probably have a little over two hours left."

She laughed. He looked troubled as he said it. "Hours? Unless that word has a much different meaning here than on my plane, I hardly think a few hours in a transport will do us harm."

"Harm, no. Boredom, yes." He closed his eyes, leaning his head back.

Cecilia realized she was still next to him on the seat, but didn't move away. Instead, she adjusted her body to mimic his pose. "You didn't find me so boring back at Central Hospital."

"That was before you slapped me," he answered. "You weren't boring when you were kissing me."

"You took liberties."

"Yes." He grinned. "I did and you enjoyed it."

His expression was slightly infuriating and yet sexy at the same time. "I suppose we could talk about what is going to happen while I'm here."

"We could. Or you could kiss me again."

Cecilia felt his heat radiating down her side. She was very aware of where his sleeve brushed against hers. Her nerves seemed to stand on end, reaching for the next light contact. "You kissed me."

Cecilia wasn't sure what made her debate him, or even talk about it. Maybe it was the new plane, the isolation of the transport and surrounding location, the subtle scent of his flesh, the heat from his body, or maybe it was the unexplainable rush of attraction that seemed to seize hold of her to the core. Doubts filled her. What if people found out? What if he told the other doctors and they didn't take her seriously? What if the tension knotting her stomach didn't go away and she was left with a sick feeling and bad memories of her time in this other world?

"I assure you, Doctor, you'll know when I kiss you."

"Why? You'll give me notice in writing?" he teased, not bothering to open his eyes.

Not knowing what exactly fueled her into action, Cecilia pushed up and leaned over him. He barely had time to look at her before she grabbed the sides of his face and kissed him. A low moan of surprise escaped him, as if he'd only been bantering with her and was stunned by her actions. For a moment, he didn't move. Then, slowly, a hand crept over her hip, testing the breadth of her resolve with that one touch.

"There are no, ah, recording devices of any kind in here, are there?" she asked when she pulled away, glancing around. Her lips tasted of him and she was breathing hard. She was in spontaneously unfamiliar territory but she didn't want this moment of insanity to come back and haunt her later. "No one is watching or listening?"

"No one." Gerard breathed just as hard. "Our trip is logged. If we do not arrive they will send help. If we need help before then we can trigger an alarm. There is an emergency medical kit on board, so you have nothing to worry about—"

Cecilia kissed him again, quieting his words. If they only had a few hours, she wanted to take full advantage of it.

"Otherwise, we are completely isolated," he

continued, as if not really paying attention to his words. His eyes roamed over her body.

"When we step out of this transport, this never happened," Cecilia said. "Agreed?"

He met her eyes and hesitated before nodding once.

"Good." This time Cecilia let her tongue slide slowly along the seam of his mouth. His hands ran along her back, exploring the line of stitching along her spine. She unfastened his long coat, pushing the material off his shoulders. The thin undershirt he wore molded to his chest. He looked to be in fine shape, but then everyone on this plane looked to be in fine shape—even that politician they called the Medical Supreme. Politicians on her plane tended to be a bit more on the gluttonous side. These people had to have some kind of easy fitness secret. If she discovered that little gem, Politician Shinclus would probably assign her to the highest medical councils. She'd have her pick of jobs.

Why was she thinking of Shinclus at a time like this?

Cecilia pulled back, feasting her eyes on the man before her.

"What is it?" he asked.

"Nothing." She pulled her clothes off her shoulders and tugged the one-piece suit down around her hips before standing to finish undressing the rest of the way. Gerard followed her example, shrugging out of his coat. His undershirt was longer at each hip than at the stomach. He grabbed the sides and slowly peeled the material off his muscled chest.

The transport turned again before building speed. Trees blurred as they zipped past. Despite this, the ride became smooth and even as if the vehicle stood perfectly still.

Naked, she came over him, straddling his body. He still wore pants, but the unmistakable outline of his cock greeted her. It brushed against her pussy, causing a shiver of anticipation to run through her. Gerard caressed her arms, reaching upward to cup her face and pull her mouth back to his. At least kissing seemed to bring them both the same kind of pleasure. If she closed her eyes, this plane almost felt normal.

The smell of him was muskier than the sweet sanitized air. She leaned in, breathing deeply, enjoying it. Heat radiated from his body, centering down between her spread legs. A small fear crept into the back of her mind. What if he wasn't built like the men she was used to? Curious, and a bit apprehensive, she brought herself more fully against his pants. He groaned. The thick arousal felt normal. Actually, it felt...

Cecilia rubbed more fully against it. The firm length stroked her clit. She'd been so tense. The pressure of this trip had been building inside her. Now that the travel was over and she was here, that tension came rolling out of her. Everything inside of her became primitive and instinctual. She wanted him on the basest of levels, a place beyond reason and logic. Her body ached, needing to be filled.

They didn't speak, even as their lips pulled apart. He touched her everywhere his hands could reach. He kissed her neck, moaned into her chest.

She threaded her fingers through his thick hair, jerking his head back. Cecilia licked at his neck, tasting his flesh. He smelled so clean, yet very masculine. Beneath her, his thighs flexed. Gerard lifted from the seat and tugged the pants from his hips. She instantly reached between their bodies to examine him, to see if he was shaped as she knew men to be. This would be an awkward encounter if she found out he had hard spikes on his penis or some kind of abnormality. Pleased, she discovered the smooth length of his arousal filled her hand. She sighed heavily in relief.

Boldly, she stroked him, massaging the full length

of his member. He adjusted his hips. The seats didn't allow for the kind of exploration she wanted.

Cecilia lifted over him and angled his cock toward her. She paused. "We're given birth control on my plane and my health checkup is clean."

"You were scanned when you entered. I'm not worried." He leaned toward the control panel. "I can show you my health scans. I'm—"

"I trust you." She pushed down onto his lap. "You are all health obsessed."

"Obsessed?" His handsome face captured her attention—the straight line of his nose, the firmness of his perfect mouth.

"Focused," she amended, needing him too urgently to argue over word choice. Cecilia wanted him inside of her. Pushing down more, she slid fully onto his naked shaft and moaned as the thick length of his cock stretched her pussy. It had been so long since she'd been sexually gratified, and it had never felt like this.

Cecilia gasped and trembled, keeping him deep even as her legs strained. She moved over him and the pleasure outweighed the discomfort of their position. She needed this too badly.

Gripping her hips, he helped to control the rhythm. He whispered something, but she couldn't make out the words. Her heart pounded heavily. She lifted and fell, pressing down hard and fast. In and out, in and out, they set a desperate rhythm. The transport turned, rocking her on top of him. The stimulation caused her to jerk. Gerard pressed her to the side, mimicking the movement. She jerked again, stiffening as he hit sweetly inside her pussy.

His feet braced the floor and he pressed up. She couldn't fight it. Her release came in a hard, ungraceful, stiffening jerk of muscles. Even her toes curled. She couldn't control her body. Gerard didn't appear to notice as he too came, finding release deep inside of her.

When his hands slipped from her hips, she fell back onto her seat. The slick material stuck to her ass. For a long moment, she didn't move, simply gasped for air.

GERARD's entire body hummed with energy. He hadn't expected such a reaction from the woman. Sure, as a man, he had hoped something would happen between them. She was a very attractive specimen of female kind, after all. What man wouldn't want to fuck that?

But it was more than a simple attraction. He felt a connection to her. It burned deep inside of him. It was impossible to explain, especially after such a short time together. Perhaps it was her eyes. She tried so hard to look calm and controlled, but he had the impression it was all an act. The way she kissed him proved there was more to this woman than her anti-chaos regulations and rigid way of talking. The coldness she exuded when she arrived he could well attribute to nerves. Gerard had seen her monitor readings. Her heart had been hammering out of control.

He smiled at her, liking the way she lounged naked, unashamed of her form. Not that she had a reason to be. She was beautiful, by any plane's standards. It was on his lips to tell her as much when she spoke first.

"You must emit some kind of pheromone," Cecilia said, as reasoning slowly came back to her. "That is the only explanation for it."

"The only?" he repeated, a little shocked by her tone. The cool dismissiveness of it didn't match the passion of moments before. She reached for her clothes and started to dress. He pulled his pants up to cover his waist. "Yes. Pheromones are a natural part of attraction." It was true, but it wasn't what he wanted to say. What he felt in those moments of pleasure went well beyond simple pheromone attraction.

"You remember our agreement? No one knows of this. What just happened between us," she gave him a pointed look, "never happened."

He nodded, hurt by the matter-of-fact tone.

"I didn't mean it like..." Cecilia hesitated.

The vulnerability was back in her eyes and she fought so hard to be in control. He felt a little sorry for her. It must be difficult trying to be so good all the time. Life on his plane was controlled, everyone was a doctor and followed protocols, but her world must be stringent if she was so terrified of anyone knowing they had sex.

"I'm a dignitary and I don't want anyone knowing that we came together in such an inappropriate way," she explained, needlessly. "I should have demanded you sign a consent form. I didn't even bring consent forms. If anyone finds out, I'll... It should not have happened. It's either pheromones, or a side effect of plane travel, I'm not sure, but whatever it is, it will not be happening again. I can't let it."

"And I am your host. I assure you, it is not in my best interest to make this known either." It was a lie. No one would care. Sex was sex. Humans had needs, and fulfilling those sexual needs was actually good for your health. As long as the dignitary was willing, he could fuck her as often as they wanted and none from his world would so much as lift a brow.

Yet, her stinging dismissal of him, of what they shared, caused him to lie. He hated lying, hated himself a little for letting it slip past his lips. Her words had been a defense. Gerard knew that and could even understand and sympathize with it. Knowing did not make it easier. So, doing what he did best, he pasted on an easy smile as he righted his clothing and pretended as if nothing in all the known planes mattered.

8

"Welcome to Biosphacility Three. It is the largest biosphere facility on our plane and where you will be working while you are here. Computers have complete access to all public records and this place is equipped with some of our most advanced technologies. You will be permitted to work and learn. A laboratory has been cleared in anticipation of your arrival." Gerard spoke, but did not lean up from his seat. "For the first month you will work in the laboratory and with the public records. In the second month, if a doctor in a field of interest is available, you will be permitted to tour the biosphacility research labs and observe experiments." He gave a small yawn. "May your stay on our plane be productive and educational, and may it lead to many future dealings between our people."

Cecilia had the impression he'd made that speech before. He glanced at her, smiling easily as if nothing had transpired between them. Okay, she knew what she had said to him and his actions were in accordance with the discretion she'd demanded from him. Even so, the emotional woman inside her began to feel a little used. The logical doctor slapped the emotional woman and reminded her that this was how things had to be. She didn't need coddling by her one-time lover. In fact, she needed him to remain professional. The easy, carefree smile was hardly professional as she would define it, but at least he wasn't pawing her and acting like they were a couple.

Pawing. She closed her eyes and took a deep breath. The feel of his hands was still burned into her flesh. If anyone found out, she could be arrested or fired. She would definitely be censured. The embarrassment of law-breaking would be mortifying. "I assume now that you have escorted me here, you will be leaving?"

The words were colder than she'd intended, and almost a little desperate. How was she supposed to concentrate around him, knowing him as intimately as she now did? What in the name of anti-chaos had she been thinking?

"No, sorry, you're stuck with me." The words were light and his smile never wavered. She looked back out the window. In the trees she saw people wearing large white suits over their entire bodies. They touched leaves with gloved hands and picked plant samples off the ground to put into specimen containers. They worked leisurely, unfazed by the transport coming past. Behind them a robotic unit lifted a scientist into the taller trees to collect from the dense tree tops. The figure disappeared into the high branches. As the transporter turned, she could no longer see them.

A glance at the man beside her was a mistake. He watched her through shaded eyes. A tiny shiver of desire went through her. She needed out of the enclosed space. Her fingers skimmed the window, already knowing there was no way to open it. They were sealed inside. No wonder she couldn't fight her desires. She was locked in a box with his pheromones.

As they turned, she was able to see the biosphacility. It curved high from the ground in a large dome surrounded a good distance away by high security gates constructed of a ring of solid stone topped by several rows of thick metal bars. Covered walkways snaked out from the center facility toward the gates like tentacles, releasing into the surrounding forest. They moved down an incline and the view became blocked by the wall.

"Are we in danger?" The transport stopped and made a series of fast beeps. The gate slid open just enough to let them slip through the wall. For a moment the transport became dark as the moved into the biosphacility. "What exactly is this wall meant to keep out?"

"Nature," he said. "The magnetic fields above keep out birds and insects. The thick wall keeps out other forest creatures. Sterilization protocols deal with any pollens and things we can't see."

An uneasiness crept through her. She felt isolated in this place. If they had to wear suits into the forest, and they were worried about whatever was in the forest getting in, she was going to be trapped there until they took her home. The more fearful she became, the more self-disciplined she tried to make herself appear. She had to maintain at least the façade of control. Her people expected her to represent them properly. It wasn't as if her travel companion Linnea was going to be much help in the inter-dimensional dignitary department when it came to representing their people.

Inside, the ground was covered with loose stones. A strange wave started under them, running in a foot-wide strip along the ground to the gate and then came back to the facility. The movement seemed to be rotating the stones on the ground and evening out the mark of footsteps. The transport drew them closer to the dome. For as large as this place was, it felt very, very small. She took a deep breath. This was her home for the next few months.

The transport stopped and the door automatically slid open. Gerard moved from his seat, hopping through the door onto the ground. He turned, offering his hand. She didn't take it, afraid of what she would feel if she touched him. Instead, she used the steps that slid out from the unit. When she vacated, the transport shut and slid along its way toward the biosphacility gate. She watched it briefly before turning her attention to her temporary home.

GERARD DIDN'T WAIT for Dr. Markos to examine the entire building, not that there was much to look at beyond the white, shiny plates of the exterior walls. Just being around her was hard, and not just hard on his emotional well-being, but damned hard on his throbbing cock. One fuck hadn't been enough, but he'd been unwilling to try for a round two when she'd hardened toward him as she did. Now, she barely looked at him, treating him like a complete stranger. Okay, so he was a stranger, technically, but they'd fucked. The least she could do was acknowledge what was between them.

Even as her cold demeanor irritated him, it made him want her all the more. He wanted to see her face soften again in passion. He wanted to push her to her knees and watch her take him into her mouth. He wanted to drag her to the nearest laboratory, bend her over a worktable and pound her hard until ever last bit of cum drained out of his cock.

He widened his easy smile and continued down the long, metal corridor. Doors lined each side. Bringing her into section one, he paused by a laboratory's entryway. "This will be where you work."

She leaned past him, careful not to touch. A few of the facility staff came down the hall. They paused, curiously eyeing their newest guest.

"Dr. Markos," Gerard automatically introduced. "This is Dr. Sunn, Dr. Frank, Dr. Jonns. Doctors, this is Dr. Cecilia Markos from New Order Society, Dimensional Plane 303. She is here to study."

"Ah, initial contact," Dr. Candra Sunn said, dismissively. She didn't think much of most inter-dimensional dignitaries and found them useless because only rarely could they provide their world with any kind of real medical advancements. She often vocally spoke out against teaching their secrets to so many other planes. "We will not be seeing each other again. I return to my arctic facility today." Then, to Gerard, she added, "I will stop by before I go." Though her tone gave nothing away, she glanced meaningfully at the clipboard she carried. She was probably reading his arousal levels and offering to take care of him before she left. The woman had sucked him off a couple times, and was quite good at it, but he didn't feel like taking her up on it this time. No, he wanted Cecilia on her knees begging for it. Without further acknowledging Cecilia, Dr. Sunn continued along her way.

Frank and Jonns were more polite. Cecilia smiled at them, warmly took their hands in greeting, and even invited them to her assigned laboratory any time they wanted. Gerard stiffened, jealous. Franks clearly took her to mean more than she had been offering—at least she had better not be offering sex to the man. Jonns appeared interested as well. If this woman thought she was going to sample her way around the men, she had another think coming.

Where was all this possessiveness coming from? His testosterone levels were way out of control. He blamed all the fantasizing he'd been doing about off-plane women since attending Sebastjan's wedding.

He waited while Cecilia went into her lab to look around. He pointed out a few of the devices before handing her a training clipboard. "If you read this, it will tell you everything you need to know about running the devices and will allow you to access any information you desire."

She took it. "Thank you."

"I'll show you to your private quarters. Your luggage should already be there." He didn't wait to see if she would follow. If he couldn't live out the fantasies pounding in his brain, he needed to get away from her to clear his mind. The wide hall split off into a narrower one which would lead to private quarters.

He stopped at her door and waited for it to slide open. The smooth walls of the chamber held no decoration, nothing that would set it apart from any other room on dimensional plane 187. A thick mattress with silver covers had been placed on the platform in the middle of the room. A health monitor turned on with the lights. There was a small area for personal needs, a row of drawers built into the wall, and items to cover every basic necessity she might have. The dark red of her bags stood out against the monochromatic interior so there was no need for him to point them out.

Stepping inside, he said, "You sleep here. Settle in however you like, read through some of the tutorials and I will be back later to bring you to the daily sustenance."

"Thank you." She stepped around him, keeping her distance as if she thought he might grab her.

Gerard turned abruptly and left, unable to stand being in her frustrating presence a moment longer.

Cecilia was finding it much harder to act controlled than she would have preferred. How did Gerard do it? Smiling as if he was completely unaffected by what they'd done. Was fucking dignitaries a normal thing for him? And why did she care?

Oh, yeah, because she was so hot she wanted nothing more than to tear off his clothes and go for a round two...and three...and four...and...

Cecilia groaned. The door slid shut behind her and she hoped it would stay that way. She dropped the electronic clipboard on the bed. Her clothes had the faint scent of sex on them, or at least she imagined they did. She pulled out of the one-piece suit, feeling as if the material was an extension of his hands on her body.

Her sex ached, begging for another climax. It would be so easy to slide a finger inside her wet pussy, though she knew that would hardly satisfy what she needed. Instead, she began opening drawers and digging through the contents. Some she could speculate as to their purpose, other objects were foreign contraptions she didn't even want to guess at. Finding a set of local garb, she tugged the material on, figuring it would be best for her to blend in. Then, still aching, she sat on the bed and began figuring out how to run the electronic clipboard. She was there to work and that was exactly what she was going to do. Hopefully, these two months would pass by quickly and if she tried really hard, she could avoid Dr. Gerard Fauchet.

10

CECILIA CLOSED her eyes and pressed her fingers to her temples. Two weeks of staring at the electronic clipboard, trying to translate what equated to some kind of ancient medical cipher, had caused a dull ache all the prescribed shots in the neck couldn't seem to get rid of. Even as she thought it, the wall monitor dinged for her attention. She glanced at it and frowned. Apparently it had read her headache and had dispatched another prescription. She knew from past attempts if she didn't take the medicine they would send someone to check on her, reciting something about protocol. Still, she didn't move. She wanted to figure out their basic formula for curing seasonal illnesses.

"Can you shut that off?" Cecilia's tone was more

of an order than a question. Linnea glanced at her from where she stared at a handheld unit and nodded. The assistant went to the wall monitor and punched in a dismissal code. The woman didn't speak much, at least not to Cecilia. When Linnea wasn't performing a required task, she was reading.

The laboratory was spacious, more so that her private quarters. She'd managed to figure out most of the equipment. Though much different in design, it functioned a lot like the technology on her plane did —only more advanced. There were work tables, dozens of pieces of medical testing equipment and sterile tubes lining one of the walls. In the corner there was a sleeping cot.

The laboratory door opened and Dr. Franks appeared. He smiled, holding up a shot. "I'm here to administer your medicine. The computer sent me an alert."

"That's not all he's here to administer," Linnea mumbled as she walked back to her seat to resume reading.

Cecilia ignored her. She much preferred when the woman didn't speak. Every word that came from Linnea's mouth seemed to drip with sarcasm. Though, in this instance, Linnea did have a small point. Dr. Franks had made his intentions toward her very known and her gentle rebuttals had met with friendly ignorance. His eyes invited her attentions. However, whereas Franks was a very attractive man, she couldn't help thinking of Gerard Fauchet.

It wasn't lost on her that she'd been determined to avoid Dr. Fauchet when she'd arrived at the biosphacility. At the time, she'd thought it would be difficult. However, as days turned to weeks and she didn't see him, she was beginning to feel slighted. How could she pointedly ignore a man who didn't show himself?

Then there were the nights—the long, long nights. Alone in her quarters, the work done for the day, all she could think about was the transporter. Strong chest. Firm flesh. Gripping hands. Heavy breath. Thick, pounding coc—

"Doctor?" Franks asked.

Cecilia blinked, realizing she'd begun daydreaming of Gerard during the day now. Heat warmed her features and she found it hard to recover her self-control. "Sorry? I'm in the middle of..." She held up an electronic clipboard, completely unable to recall what she'd been reading moments before.

"I understand," Franks said, lifting the shot. She leaned her head to the side to give him access to her neck and closed her eyes. He gave her a quick injection. It did lessen her headache. He then deposited the dispenser into the wall unit to be sanitized. "Perhaps we can talk later, after you're done with your work?"

Linnea gave a small laugh. Both doctors turned to her. She held up her clipboard and motioned to its contents. "Funny stuff."

"Perhaps," Cecilia said, "but there is a lot for me to learn and only a couple of months for me to do it in."

Franks grinned, clearly taking her words to mean there was hope for his suit. She sighed as he left, only to stiffen as the object of her desires entered. Gerard was the last person she'd expected to see. For a moment, she blinked, thinking she hallucinated him. When he didn't disappear, she gave a slight nod.

"I've come to see how things are progressing. My reports say you've accessed many of the public databases." Gerard's voice was low. Even though his easy smile gave her no hope of a repeated transporter trip, she couldn't help the shiver of anticipation and longing that filtered through her. She'd had time to think and was a little ashamed she'd been so quick to deny what had happened.

"I wouldn't say *many*," Cecilia said, glancing at her work. Was he having fun at her expense? She'd only accessed a couple of the basics and was still trying to figure out equivalent expressions for the same things on her plane. "But I'm managing."

Linnea cleared her throat and stood. She held her clipboard to her chest. "If you no longer need me?"

"Yes, fine," Cecilia dismissed. Her assistant left.

When they were alone, he continued, "The reports also say you've had several headache injections since I've been gone. I've come to see if you have an underlying medical problem. Are such headaches normal?"

"You were gone?" she asked, surprised. That would explain why she hadn't seen him. She'd thought he'd been staying away from her because she'd told him to. Almost every day she'd regretted it.

"Didn't someone tell you? I was called back to Asclepius by Dr. Lu. There was a matter that needed my attention." Gerard's eyes dipped, not meeting hers.

"Asclepius?" Cecilia put the clipboard down and took several steps toward him. She breathed rapidly. "It's not the portal, is it? We're not...?"

"Trapped?" he finished for her. "No, it's not the portal. It was a medical issue."

"Oh." Cecilia felt a little silly for her panic. "I hope everything worked out favorably?"

"Not yet. Hopefully soon." His tone dismissed the subject. "We were discussing your head."

This was not the conversation she wanted to have, but she was unsure how to start something more intimate. "They're tension headaches, nothing more. There is a lot of information to absorb and very little time to do it. I was hoping that you would let me bring the files home with me to further study—"

"Let me stop you there. No, I apologize, but our medical knowledge does not leave our plane. It is the law. You are welcome to the public information while you're here, but anything that leaves has to be pre-negotiated between the Medical Supreme and your politicians." Gerard smiled, the irritatingly easy look she'd remembered all too often while alone in her quarters.

Cecilia knew as much. Still, she'd been instructed to try.

"Is there something I can assist you with to help with the headaches?" His smile remained intact. He went to the door and pushed the scanner next to it. The unit beeped once, indicating the door was locked.

"What are you doing, Dr. Fauchet?"

Gerard laughed. He arched a brow. "Really? You have to ask?"

"I mean, of course I know what you're doing." Cecilia became flustered and she didn't like that he could make her feel like an idiot with just one playful look. "What happened to remaining professional?"

"Most of the laboratories are closed for the night. Your assistant is gone. I can think of nothing more professional than a doctor trying to cure another doctor's headache."

The man was incorrigible, and yet she found herself unable to suppress a small laugh.

"You can't tell me you haven't considered fucking me again?" he persisted.

"I wanted to apologize for how I left things last time. I reacted badly." Cecilia had to admit his confidence was sexy. "Still, what you are suggesting is not..."

"What?" He came closer. "Please don't say prudent."

"Logical," Cecilia finished.

"Which is exactly why I prescribe it for you." He came to a stop in front of her. The smell of him was familiar. A shiver worked down her spine. Her breathing deepened. Gerard lowered his tone to a seductive whisper. "The only way to cure logic is by doing something illogical."

"They do say that doctors should never diagnose themselves." What was she doing? This man was chaos. She was about control. Still, no one would know. No one would see. He was her one chance to give in to something wild and crazy. "No one can know about this."

"You made your terms clear." Gerard pressed his mouth to hers, stopping any last-second protests she might make.

Cecilia liked to think she would have made such protests, but in truth she doubted it. The second she saw him, she wanted him again. She wanted a release from work, from feeling like a complete, inept idiot who couldn't read a basic medical book. Basic inter-dimensional communication was the same, but their advanced medical language had a nuance to it she couldn't quite grasp.

"Now let me tell you my terms," he whispered.

When she would have pulled away, he moved forward and deepened the kiss until all reason faded into that blissful moment. She grabbed his hair briefly before running her hands down to his lab coat. Eagerly she tugged it open, fumbling with the mate-rial to get to the flesh underneath. He finally let her escape his kiss. She gasped for breath. The intensity of his eyes pierced into her, holding her gaze captive. She couldn't close her eyes and she couldn't look away.

"You can keep your secret, Doctor," he allowed, "but no more denying what is between us."

Their breaths mingled, heavy, passionate pants of air. His hands artfully unfastened her lab coat to expose her skin underneath. She did not wear the customary undershirt beneath the coat, finding the practice of layering multiple pieces of clothing odd and uncomfortable.

Gerard ran his hands down her chest. He caressed her breasts, his fingers tweaking her nipples.

"And what is between us?" Cecilia asked with a small moan of pleasure. What was it about this man? She'd never reacted so strongly to a lover before.

"Passion, attraction..." He thrust his hips against her so she could feel the hard outline of his cock. "Sexual chemistry."

Sexual chemistry wasn't exactly the most romantic thing he could have said, but the way he said it caused her to shiver in anticipation. The tension eased out of her, melting away into oblivion. Even so, she refused to give over the last bit of control. She turned him so that his ass pressed against a work table.

Cecilia undressed him, freeing his cock from beneath his pants. Boldly, she stroked the length, running her hands over his shaft. His breath caught. She did it again, tightening her grip.

Gerard reached for her face, but she dodged his kiss. His lips curled up at one side in a half smile. Challenge lit in his gaze. His lab coat was open, hanging on his arms. She grabbed hold of it and pulled him with her toward a small cot in the corner of the room. When she released the material, the coat fell to the floor.

Cecilia pushed the pants from her hips, kicking them off her feet. She fell back onto the cot. Gerard followed her, naturally settling between her legs. The smooth, firm texture of his skin felt so good against her hands. She wrapped her legs around his, hooking her feet on the back of his knees to draw him forward.

"I'm going to fuck you, Cecilia," Gerard asserted boldly, "without written permission."

Cecilia moaned in response, thrilled by the naughtiness of it.

"You're my bad girl, aren't you?" Gerard kissed her.

She bit his bottom lip lightly. Her nails raked his back and he shivered, making a small noise of approval. She scratched harder while licking his lip. The hard press of his cock drew along her inner thigh. She trembled in anticipation, tensing ever so slightly while she waited for that first intimate slide of his body inside her. That first thrust did not come as hard and fast as she expected. Instead, he entered her slowly, forcing her eyes to meet his passionate gaze. "Look at me."

Cecilia obeyed. Her toes curled and she found it hard to catch her breath. He moved against her, his hips brushing her thighs before pulling back. Each movement was measured and drawn out.

There were no words, nothing beyond that look in his eyes and the feel of his body. Every part of her concentrated on him. Planes and worlds did not exist. The laboratory did not exist. Medical science, anti-chaos laws and annoying assistants did not exist. There was only now, him, this moment of perfection.

Cecilia pushed her hips, trying to force him to quicken his pace. He didn't, remaining in complete control. The rhythm was torment, sweet and utter torment. She wanted to shove him onto his back and take over, but he wouldn't obey her insistent pushes along his shoulders.

The pleasure built, racking through her body in a giant explosive release. Only after she'd found her climax did Gerard join her. He tensed, frozen at the pentacle of desire for the briefest of moments before collapsing over her.

Cecilia's bones felt as if they melted inside her body. Her legs fell limply to the sides. Gerard shielded her from his weight by bracing himself on his elbow.

"How does this keep happening?" she whispered.

He turned his face toward her neck, nuzzling her. "Simple. I'm irresistible."

She weakly hit his arm.

He pulled back, giving her the charming smile he wore so well. "Because you are irresistible."

"This can't go anywhere. As soon as my assignment here is over, I have to go home." Cecilia didn't want to face reality, but it came crashing in around them anyway.

Gerard kissed her neck and ear. "Unless your plane has some kind of future-telling ability we don't know about, you have no way of predicting what will happen. Stop trying to define everything. Just let it be what it is. Let it become what it will become."

"I need us to be honest. My plane has logic.

Logic tells me nothing will come of this. My heart tells me I don't belong here and that I want to go home. I would never be able to accept a permanent post here. I have a life on my world that I will not leave behind." Cecilia wasn't sure why she needed to make sure he understood. Maybe she needed herself to hear the words aloud.

"We don't offer permanent posts."

"My point exactly. And from what I understand of the agreement, none of your medical technology can come back. I'm assuming that includes the doctors as well. You can't come with me." She reminded herself to remain in control of her emotions. Chaos brought with it a myriad of problems. When Gerard touched her she became mindless. This second encounter proved as much.

"No. Doctors do not accept permanent posts elsewhere. Normally other planes come to us. We do not go to them." He kissed her again, sending shivers over her. "But there is no reason for you not to have some fun while you're here."

Beyond the way he made her feel, the only thing she knew of this man came from how those at the biosphacility spoke of him. They respected him, that much was clear, but there was little said beyond that.

"It's late and I have a lot of reading left to do tonight." She pushed at his shoulder.

"Are you sure? I could follow you back to your quarters." He let her guide him up.

"Linnea is going to meet me there later to finish up our logs," she lied. She moved to gather her clothing, glancing at the door. It was locked, but that didn't stop her from thinking someone might come in and catch them.

"That is unfortunate. Though I suppose there are things I should attend to. There will be plenty of paperwork to sign from my absence." He stood, pulling on his lab coat. "However, now that I'm back I'm sure we'll be seeing much more of each other. I'll come by tomorrow evening. Try not to make plans with Linnea."

Cecilia was much slower to move as she fastened her coat. He waited while she righted her clothing. Then, coming to her, he gently kissed her mouth and caressed her cheek.

"Dream well, Dr. Markos," he whispered.

Cecilia watched him go, trying to look calm. Inside, her emotions erupted into chaos.

11

GERARD HAD NOT PLANNED on making love to Cecilia again. Yes, he'd thought about her endlessly while away, but he hadn't expected a repeat of their time in the transport. There was just something about her that drew him to her and silently begged for his kisses. He felt the pull as strongly as that first moment, if not more so. Even now he tasted her on his lips.

But her shame of their sexual encounters had not changed. Why was he doing this to himself? She was right. There was no future in it.

It didn't matter. He was taken by her and he would go back to her again and again, as often as she would have him, until their story together came to an end.

"Dr. Fauchet, I heard you had returned. What news? Is it true? Has there been an outbreak?"

Gerard frowned, quickly glancing behind him to make sure no one heard Dr. Jonns's panicked questions. He was under strict orders that no outsiders should know of their situation. Dr. Jonns only knew because he'd intercepted a message meant for Dr. Swift. Unfortunately, the man's level of panic would only be magnified if the full truth were known. Jonns wasn't exactly the most composed of researchers, preferring botany science and food production to human infectious diseases even though he was technically qualified to help with the problem. Should others find out before they had more facts, there would be worldwide terror. With their medical advancements came a false sense of security that they could cure anything.

"No. There is no outbreak," Gerard assured the man.

Jonns did not look fully convinced. "Then the illness is contained? How many infected? What is it?" Looking at Gerard, he stepped back. He glanced up at the wall monitor, as if Gerard himself might be carrying a new virus.

Gerard lifted up his hands. "I'm clean. I've been scanned many times."

Jonns nodded, but did not reclose the distance between them.

"Privacy Code Six has been enacted. We're not allowed to discuss it with anyone. Since you're privy to the information, you will be tasked as one of the members working to find out what it is we're dealing with. Currently, there is only one infected, but we're concerned the virus is airborne. Sanitation protocols have been enacted as well."

"Who? Who is infected? A traveler? Are they quarantined? What about the portal? Have they suspended travel?"

Gerard heard the door behind him and gestured Jonns to hurry down the hall. They ducked into an empty laboratory. Seconds later, Cecilia walked by the door. She did not look in.

"Is it..?" Jonns motioned toward the door in horror. "Dr. Markos and Sans Nel? They're the carriers, are they?"

"No." That was the last rumor Gerard wanted circulating around amongst his peers. If Jonns thought the virus was inside the local facility, the man wouldn't be able to keep his mouth shut about it. "I am not at liberty to discuss the patient, but he is local. You will get a copy of the report. Dr. Swift will personally deliver the information when it is ready.

Until then, you are to clear your cases and prepare a private laboratory to work. Assign your current projects to another doctor. This is top priority."

Jonns nodded in understanding. "It is one of the facility directors, isn't it? They're always overseeing experiments they shouldn't be." The man was merely guessing. "Dr. Sebastian Walter? The Medical Supreme's son? That's why the secrecy. Or Dr. Hattu? They found something at the underwater biosphacility. They're always bringing up samples they should leave on the ocean floor."

Gerard was careful not to give anything away with his expression. "I cannot say more."

Jonns gave him a knowing look, though Gerard doubted the man knew the full extent of what they were dealing with. In truth, Jonns was not the man Gerard would have picked for this job. But it wasn't his decision. It was Swift's.

"You have your orders, Doctor." Gerard reached to open the door. He glanced out, making sure the halls were empty. His eyes lingered in the direction where Cecilia disappeared. "And I have a stack of paperwork waiting for me."

GERARD HAD COME AS PROMISED that first night, and every night since. Cecilia found herself looking forward to his visits, even going so far as to send Linnea away early. He never said much, beyond the charming nothings that seemed to come so easily for him. He asked if she needed supplies, if the food was to her liking, if she wanted to let him follow her back to her quarters to stay the night. The laboratory was well stocked, the food was bland but palatable—not that she told him as much—and the answer to his last question was always, "No. I have much work to do."

Passion wasn't a problem. One look, one touch, one kiss and she fell willingly into his arms. The problem came afterward, when she watched him leave, and she realized each night she fell deeper and deeper into chaos. The more she was with him, the more she thought about him when he was away. Her mind drifted from her work. Every nerve ending tingled until the damned wall monitor beeped and forced her to take shots for her levels.

"Levels," she muttered. Half the time she didn't understand what the unbalanced levels were that the computer was telling her to fix. If the desire stirred too fierce, a shot to the neck numbed it back to manageable levels.

Cecilia rubbed her neck. She was really tired of injections. As if on cue, the wall monitor beeped. Frustrated, she grabbed the electronic syringe, pressed it to the wall unit and stuck it in her neck. The knot in her stomach eased, but it was just a physical relief, not a mental one. The stress remained.

There was one very glaringly obvious fact about this plane—citizens were obsessed with immortality. There were numerous references to the pursuit of escaping death. Some tried to find the path to ascension, electrocuting themselves in the process, the rest of them just tried to cure everything and block out what they couldn't.

She looked up at the ceiling. They'd been trapped inside since they arrived.

"Over half," Linnea said. The woman hardly

ever spoke to her but when she did the words were tipped with an emotion akin to indifference.

"Half of what?" Cecilia asked.

"You were mumbling out loud again," Linnea said, not glancing up from her work. "You said we were almost halfway done. In fact, we are over halfway done. As of yesterday, we are starting month two."

"It's this place. With no daylight, it's impossible to keep track of the hours." Cecilia studied the woman, part of her wishing Linnea was someone else, part of her wishing Linnea would look up and smile at her in some kind of same-plane camaraderie.

Linnea did look up, but it wasn't to smile. "Go up to the top level. There's plenty of sunlight."

"The top level?" Cecilia again looked up, as if the ceiling would part and show her something new.

"Haven't you wandered around at all?" Linnea asked.

"No. I've only gone where instructed, as should you. They showed us our quarters, the dining hall and our laboratory."

"Not surprising this," Linnea drawled. "You're one of those true believers in the anti-chaos, aren't you? One of the devout."

"No," Cecilia denied, not liking the comparison to being a monk.

"Really? Then why all the shame about Dr. Fauchet?" Linnea chuckled.

Cecilia stiffened. "I don't know what you mean."

"All right then. Whatever you say, Doctor." Linnea laughed harder. "It's about time for you to kick me out for your..." The woman paused, giving her a meaningful look. "Your nightly serious platonic anti-chaos discussions with Dr. Fauchet."

Cecilia felt heat rising to her cheeks at the sarcastic tone. "My professional medical conversations with Dr. Fauchet, our inter-dimensional contact, are not of your concern. You haven't been to medical school, so I understand you have no idea the level of complicated maneuvering and paperwork involved in a mission such as ours."

Linnea set down her electronic clipboard and moved toward the door. "A little hint, Doctor." She ran her hand over the wall unit and smiled. It wasn't lost on Cecilia that she'd been wishing for that very look just moments before. Now she wished it would go away. Linnea's smiles weren't comforting. "As you've pointed out on many occasions, I'm not a doctor, but in my experience, anti-chaos conversations work much better if you keep your clothes on."

The woman left and seconds later the wall unit beeped for her to correct her levels. Cecilia glared at the monitor. Linnea's words left her mortified. Everywhere she looked reminded her of making love to Gerard. Perhaps having an affair inside her laboratory wasn't the best of ideas.

Instead of correcting anything, she slammed her hand against the counter and stormed out of the laboratory. She wanted to be in control. There was comfort in control. Control was safe and good and right and...

Her breathing deepened. She needed to monitor her emotional output. If she kept on as she was, in a month she'd be an embarrassing wreck returning home. Cecilia wasn't sure where to go. She couldn't be in the laboratory and she couldn't roam the areas of the biosphacility where she'd not been explicitly told she could venture.

Her feet carried her to her private quarters. Perhaps it was best she hid where no one could see her. Once inside, she paced the floor like a caged animal.

A strange beep sounded by the door. She ignored it. It was probably just a warning to take her shot. Seconds later the door slid open.

She inhaled sharply and turned, lifting her arms up in fright.

"What's happening?" Gerard asked, coming in without being invited.

"I locked the door." Cecilia pointed at the monitor.

"And I overrode the lock," he explained. "Now, what is happening? The computer said you were agitated and that you did not take your shot. Are you ill? What are you feeling?"

"You need to go. I can't concentrate when you're near." She waved him away when he stepped closer. "I need to concentrate. My assistant hates me, which is fine, because she's rude and sarcastic, but she's not a doctor so I can't really discuss medical stuff with her beyond telling her what to log for our paperwork. Your plane's medical knowledge is so vast, yet I'm still stuck trying to decipher that what we call Firghelm Syndrome you call Policompititen-something."

"Policompition Ten," he supplied.

"Yes, that!" She resumed her pacing. "We cured Firghelm years ago, but I just spent a day translating your documents to try to understand what I was looking at, only to discover it was chronic itchy feet. I thought it was the basic formula for curing seasonal illnesses. But no, itchy feet."

He smiled that damned charming look that made her all tingly. Her frown deepened.

"There is no way I'm going to get much past the basics at the rate I'm going," she continued. "My government is depending on me to bring back something fabulous. If I don't, I could very well lose my job, or if I'm lucky, simply be demoted. What is worse, if that happens, I can't tell people why. I can't say, well I was in an alternate reality and only given two months to conquer the impossible task of trying to learn a new language and get a secondary medical degree. They'll think I'm insane." Cecilia turned her attention to Gerard. "Then there is you. You make me all chaotic inside."

"Cecilia, take a breath." He reached into his pocket and pulled out an electronic syringe. He leaned toward her and injected her before she had time to swat his hand away. He dropped the syringe in a nearby disposal. "Better?"

Yes, she did feel better physically. She felt calmer and able to focus. However, warmth flowed through her veins, unlike the previous injections, giving her the sensation of being tipsy. "You shouldn't be in here."

"Neither should you." His hand brushed her cheek. "We had a meeting scheduled in your laboratory. I was looking forward to it. Seeing you is the highlight to my day."

A shiver worked over her. She couldn't pull herself away from him. His eyes held such emotion, beautiful and passionate. His charming smile drew her closer. This man had a power about him. If she believed in magic, she would have called it that.

Gerard fingered a strand of her hair. His eyes stayed on hers, as if something about her fascinated him. Heat built inside her. Electricity snapped between them, silent, invisible and strong. It always happened like this. Whenever he was near, she was pulled deeper and deeper into his chaos.

There was a surety to his actions she did not have. He knew what he wanted and wasn't ashamed of taking it. The backs of his fingers fell against her neck. The hair he held tickled her as he drew a line down the neckline of her lab coat. The lock slipped from his grasp and he turned his hand to begin unfastening the coat.

"I enjoy your smell," he whispered. "Is it a special scent from your home plane?"

"It is government-approved soap," she answered. "All citizens are issued the same kind."

He breathed deeply and sighed. "I like it."

Gerard's hand brushed over her naked breast as he continued unfastening the coat. The action caused her nipple to tighten in anticipation. As the material was lifted from her skin, the cool room air puckered her flesh, erecting the tiny hairs.

"Some planes call horripilation bird flesh." He hummed thoughtfully and lightly touched her chest. "Or goosebumps."

"How do you keep all the words in your head?" Her mind followed the path of his fingers instead of concentrating fully on his words.

"They say I have a talent for languages. If I read it, the words seem to stay in my head."

"I hate feeling stupid."

"No one here thinks you're stupid. The fact that your plane trusted you enough to send you here proves your intelligence." Then louder, he added, "Computer, dim lights."

The lights dimmed in the room. She gasped, looking up. "They didn't tell me the room was voice activated."

"It's in the tutorials file package you received on the handheld when you arrived." His lips swept along hers.

"The tutorials were organized horribly. The

workflow was completely sideways compared to what I'm used to."

He chuckled.

"I shouldn't complain," she amended quickly. "On behalf of my plane, we are very grateful for this opportunity to learn from you and I will try harder and work longer hours."

"Shh," Gerard urged. "Try to quiet your mind. Thinking about something too hard makes it harder to understand."

Shadows cast over his features. His words drew her full attention to his face while he undressed her. Her clothes slipped easily off her body. He ran his hands down the small of her back, over the curve of her ass. When she stood completely naked, he stepped back, studying her form.

Gerard leisurely pulled off his clothes, letting her watch. His fingers followed the stripe on his coat, unfastening the hidden buttons. She licked her lips in anticipation, watching the show of flesh unfold. His erection lifted his pants. He pulled the waist-band forward, freeing his cock.

She moved to her bed and lay on her back. Naked, he crawled over her. She lifted her arms to accept him and her hands glided over his strong chest, rising and falling along the ridges of his muscles. The intimacy of the dimmed light contrasted that of the bright laboratory. Her eyes caressed him, following her hands.

Gerard settled between her legs. His hips forced them open. The hard length of his arousal stroked along the wet folds of her pussy. He parted his lips and his mouth hovered over hers. A light moan escaped her, turning into a gasp when he pressed his hips more firmly against her.

Fingers skimmed her nipples before making their way down her stomach. He gently opened the lips of her sex, readying her body to take his. She tensed, taking his breath into her lungs as she waited for that perfect moment.

Gerard's mouth claimed hers as he thrust forward. His tongue glided through her lips as his cock entered her sex. He braced his weight to the side as he moved within her. His free hand found her breast, massaging the globe deeply. He rocked his hips against her and soon the steady rhythm became frantic and pounding. Their limbs tangled in a series of frenzied movements. She flipped him over on his back and raked her nails down his chest. He groaned, rolling her back around to thrust harder.

Bedding bunched under her thigh and she lifted

her leg. He hooked the back of her knee with his arm. The move let him go deeper still.

"*Apolloa*, you are sweet."

"I'm Cecilia," she corrected, instantly pushing at his shoulders.

"It means goddess," he assured her, kissing her deeply before she could stop and think too much.

The pleasure built before exploding within her. She gasped and tensed as the climax overtook her body. Gerard's release joined hers. He jerked his hips, trembling violently above her.

He fell next to her on the bed. She lay beside him, relaxed and sated, not thinking, just being. That was, until he spoke.

"I am sorry the translations are proving difficult. What if we extended your visit?" he asked.

She turned her head to look at him. His face was close, his nose almost touching hers. The smell of him radiated over her. Cecilia almost said yes in a moment of weakness—yes to him, not to work. "My government would not allow it without better reason. There is protocol that must be followed to change a mission order. My people don't like surprise and change. I can't guarantee I'd find enough reason with a little extra time, unless your government would be willing to give me the answers?"

"They don't know you well enough. My government is not too trusting, especially on a first mission."

"Are you allowed to help me translate the text?" she asked. "I would appreciate the assistance."

It was hard for her to ask it. She was so used to doing things on her own, for herself. On her plane she was in a competitive field.

"I'll do what I can." Gerard pushed up and sighed. "Are you sure you won't reconsider and stay longer?"

"I told you, it's not up to me. It would take a minimum of two months to fast-track something through the government channels."

"I'm sorry to hear that." He turned his back to her.

"You knew my stay was temporary," Cecilia whispered. She reached to touch him but merely let her hand hover near his back, not making contact. "We both knew the arrangement going in."

"I'm sorry, because I was hoping you would stay voluntarily and this next conversation could be avoided." He stood and grabbed his lab coat. He slipped it over his shoulders, not bothering to put on the undershirt.

Cecilia grabbed the blankets and pulled them to her chest. "Explain yourself."

"We cannot allow you to leave our plane at this time."

"You are kidnapping us?" She pushed up from the bed. Panic filled her. The biosphacility was in the middle of their planet, far from the portal. The portal was in the middle of their most prestigious hospital, hidden by a maze of hallways. She'd never find her way back there, not without help. "Why would you do such a thing?"

"The decision has been made for reasons I cannot discuss with you. But, for the time being all inter-dimensional travel has been suspended. All dignitaries will remain at their assigned facilities until further notice." He didn't look at her so she forced him to by stepping in his way. She stared at him until his eyes met hers. "There has been a medical incident at Asclepius. Until such a time as it passes, we cannot permit any travel outside of our plane." She arched a brow, not moving. "Cecilia...Dr. Markos, please understand that this is hopefully a temporary situation and is incredibly rare. It is possible this will be resolved before you were supposed to leave."

"Possible but not likely." Her expression was stiff and her breathing too measured.

He tried to comfort her, but she saw he doubted

his own words. Her mind whirled with thoughts. A medical situation that these people were not equipped to handle? Not only was she trapped in an alien world, they were under medical containment. What if they never let her leave the biosphacility?

"Leave." Cecilia's heart beat hard in her chest.

"I told you. Not until there is portal clearance."

"Leave," she repeated. The wall monitor beeped. He lifted his hand as if to indicate she needed medicine. "I said get out of my quarters."

"Oh, you mean leave your room." He quickly pulled on his pants. Gerard paused beside the door. He opened his mouth to speak but she cut him off with a hard look as she pointed at the door in warning. He nodded once and left her alone.

Cecilia gasped for breath, trying not to cry out. Her knees weakened and she collapsed onto the bed. She panted, trying to get oxygen into her body, but she found it hard to breathe. Fear trapped her mind. She couldn't live like this, forever, here, forever...

"Forever?" She stared at the sterile walls, feeling as if they grew smaller. A couple of months was one thing, but now? She hugged her legs to her chest. "Please don't make me stay here forever."

THE RELATIONSHIP with Cecilia wasn't going according to Gerard's plan. Well, honestly, he didn't really have a plan, but if he did, this would not be it. Every time he went to her, he ran through his mind what he wanted to say to her. None of it ever made it past his lips. One look at her and every logical thought left his brain.

"I could have handled it better," he told himself, not for the first time that morning. He knew he'd said too much about their situation, but that hadn't stopped him.

"Dr. Fauchet?"

Seeing Dr. Sam Swift, Gerard turned his attention to the man. He didn't try to make excuses for why he was pacing back and forth along the long corridor. "Dr. Markos does not want to take us up on the offer to stay longer. I plan to take her outside and try again. Maybe a walk in the forest will pique her scientific interest. What about Sans Nel? Did you get a chance to talk to her last night?"

"I did. Instinct tells me they are not responsible for this." Sam hesitated. "I received a communication early this morning. The Medical Supreme's condition has worsened. A couple of his staff are now showing symptoms. It's spreading. If we can't make the dignitaries want to stay, then we have no choice but to inform them or imprison them. I have no wish to imprison them."

Gerard let loose a long breath. He didn't tell the Medical Director that he'd already told Cecilia too much the night before. For some reason he found it impossible to lie to her. "There are other options. I can break protocol and ask her to help us with this problem. Or I can show her something that is not in the public dignitary archives, something she will not be able to resist."

"The Medical Supreme will never approve opening up the secure knowledge bases to strangers. Even sick, I doubt he would give up any future bargaining chips. However, he might agree to have another doctor work on his illness. If we don't tell her it's from our plane, and we don't mention that the Medical Supreme is sick..." Sam rubbed the bridge of his nose thoughtfully. Gerard wondered at the man's tone. Sam was normally very decisive. "Let me speak with Dr. Lu."

"If it helps, Dr. Markos has accessed more of the records in a short time than most dignitaries do in most trips." He didn't mention Cecilia's doubts in her ability to understand that material.

"I remember seeing a report for her login. I didn't think her accesses high in number. In fact, I think they were average."

"Check her assistant's code," Gerard assured him. "I think she has Sans Nel bring up the reports for her."

Sam stretched his fingers wide, studying his hands. "All right. I'll discuss it with Dr. Lu."

Gerard knew that was the best answer he was going to get. In order to give her access, Dr. Swift needed a second doctor with high level clearance to sign off on the plan. "So I have your permission to take her outside?"

Sam nodded. "I'll sign off on it as soon as I get to my office."

Gerard hoped Cecilia would be agreeable. Her stress levels were getting worse and her injections more frequent. That worried him. Unlike Linnea, she didn't seem to leave the visitor's section of the facility. She needed to see there was more to his plane than labs and medical texts. The last thing he wanted was to imprison her here. If they did that, she would never forgive them, or him.

14

CECILIA BLINKED as the bright sunlight hit her face for the first time in over a month. The brightness did not bring the expected warmth, though. Inside the large, white, plastic suit her body temperature was regulated. The clear plastic shield over face separated her from the fresh air. As her eyes adjusted, she looked up at the tall trees. Behind her, the biosphacility door slid shut, closing off the maze of dim hallways they'd walked through to get to the outside border.

For a moment, she didn't move. Gerard wore a matching suit. His movements were stiff as he turned to her. When he spoke, the small click of a communicator preceded his words. "Try to breathe normally. You will get used to the suit."

"I am breathing normally," she answered, though it was a lie. Her panted breaths filled the helmet, fogging the bottom edge of the face shield.

When she moved to follow him over the dirt path, the suit swished in time with her steps. Her thighs were forced open by the bulk of the material.

"This is ridiculous," she muttered.

"What?"

"I said this is ridiculous," she stated louder.

"No," Gerard corrected, "I meant, what is it you find ridiculous?"

"What are we doing out here?" Cecilia stopped walking. She couldn't learn anything stuffed inside a human-shaped bag. "Don't we need a specimen container?"

"We're not collecting specimens," he said.

"Then what?" She was forced to continue on after him when he didn't stop moving into the forest. The trees towered over them. She glanced back at the biosphacility. It wasn't far away, but the denseness of the forest obscured it from view within a short distance. "I should get back to my work."

"It's just a little further this way," he said, waving his arm forward.

"Are you going to help me find information useful to my plane?" she asked.

"No. I told you, the Medical Supreme would never allow it."

"You're not going to..." She hesitated, trying not to give in to the thread of fear curling insider her. "Are you bringing me out here because I refused to stay longer?"

"What?" He turned sharply. His hands lifted and he jerked the helmet off his head. "You honestly think I am capable of hurting you?"

"Gerard!" Cecilia rushed forward, her heart hammering in her chest. "What are you doing? Your helmet!" She grabbed to take it from him. The gloves made her hands clumsy as she tried to lift it up over his head. "Try not to breathe."

Gerard laughed. He snatched the helmet from her hands. "I'm rather partial to breathing."

Cecilia stared at him, confused.

His laugh faded and he gave her an endearing look. "Trust me." Gerard reached for her head. She pulled back. "Cecilia, trust me."

Slowly, she nodded. He unfastened her helmet and pulled it off her head. She took a deep breath as the cool air hit her. It felt nice and fresh, more like home. The scent of trees filled her nose. She pulled at the neck of her suit, craving the feel of air on her skin. The sweet sterilizer couldn't be detected in nature, but she knew it permeated her body. She ran her fingers through her hair, pushing it back from her face.

"Why would you lock yourselves away from this?" she asked.

"Fear does many things to people. When I was a child there were still a few people who were unafraid of nature and walked in parks without the protective gear. One year the pollen count was high and set off allergies. A few people who didn't walk outside were made sick by those who did. The Medical Supreme ordered new nature protocols and it became illegal to breathe unsanitized air."

"I'm breaking the law right now?" Cecilia wasn't sure why the idea didn't terrify her as much as it should have. "Won't the orderkeepers come for us?"

He placed their helmets on the ground and began shrugging out of his protective suit. "You have nothing to fear."

"But there can be no society without control." The mantra sounded a bit hollow when she said it. "I am sure the Medical Supreme understands this and enacted the anti-chaos protocols for the good of society."

"I will tell you a secret if you promise not to repeat it." He waited for her nod of agreement. "The

Medical Supreme has some of the worst allergies I have ever seen. He was one of the few affected by the secondary pollen exposure. Instead of inconveniencing himself with daily injections, he changed medical protocol."

"He is that sort of politician." Cecilia frowned. "This is why we are suddenly trapped? Something happened to the Medical Supreme that he does not like and everyone must now bend to his whim despite the chaos it causes."

"I never said it was the Medical Supreme who was sick." The surprise in his voice at her astuteness confirmed just that.

"It's an easy deduction even if your expression did not give you away. Considering what he did over allergies, I'm not surprised he closed down a portal for whatever this new thing is that he's contracted, especially if he thinks off-plane dignitaries are to blame for bringing it." Logic did not give her comfort. "Gerard, he's not going to let us go home, is he? He's blocking the portal."

"No," he assured her. He set his suit on the ground next to the helmets. "The portal is too important to this plane. They might make the travel protocols more stringent, but they will never cut off portal travel completely. I promise you, you will see your home world again. We have some of the best minds working on a cure. You just might go home later than planned."

"I want to see the medical reports. If my going home is contingent on discovering what this is, I deserve a chance to help." She glanced at his hands as he reached for her suit. He unfastened the shoulders to help her out of it. It didn't completely register what he was doing as she was more concentrated on her predicament. "Depending on what this is, it could take months, *years*, to understand it."

The weight of the suit slid off her shoulders and she stepped out of it. Gerard motioned around them. "I thought you might like to get out of the biosphacility. Normally, I would have offered you a tour before now, but this crisis has me occupied."

"I want to help," she repeated emphatically.

"I already asked for permission, but at this point it is probably too late to stop you. I've seen the number of documents you've had your assistant access on your behalf. You must really have a grasp on our medical knowledge by now. However, I must ask you to keep your suspicions about the Medical Supreme to yourself."

"My assistant?" She frowned, confused. "I don't have Linnea access documents for me. She does a few logs. I assume she's spending most of her days reading fiction novels."

"We don't have pretend novels," he said. "I have heard of such things being popular on other planes, but here if you write fiction it is punishable by death, since faking research results is a grave offense. Our records show she's accessed several medical documents."

Cecilia wasn't sure what to say. "But...she's not a doctor."

"Should we be worried? You don't think she's doing something with the information, do you?"

"No. I don't think she..." Cecilia frowned. She didn't want to lie, but she didn't know what the truth was. "Linnea and I only met for this assignment. My people would not send someone they did not think would act as a dignitary should."

A bird call sounded over them. Gerard glanced to the trees and smiled. "Come explore with me. I brought you out here to relax, not discuss politics."

"Relax?" The concept was strange. "We're in the middle of a medical crisis and you want me to relax?"

"Nothing can be done at this moment." Gerard reached his hand out. "Walk with me. Let me show you there are things on this plane beyond laboratories and sterile rooms."

15

GERARD HAD TOLD Cecilia too much. She knew about the Medical Supreme. He told her there was a chance she could work on the medical crisis. Dr. Swift hadn't given permission for it yet. But how could he deny her? How could he lie to her? He was in love with her.

Gerard stopped walking. The sounds of the forest echoed around them. None of the scientists would be out collecting today. The solitude helped to clear his thoughts and focus his emotions. His heart beat faster in his chest. He was in love with her.

"What is it? Gerard?" Cecilia touched him. The press of her fingers to his arm was like shot of the best illegal pleasure drugs.

"I would have to check my levels with a monitor

to prove it to you, but I am certain." He covered her hand with his.

"Certain—?"

"I love you, Cecilia. I am in love with you. I—"

"You love me?" She cut off his decree. "This isn't logical. We don't even exist on each other's worlds. I shouldn't even be here. Sometimes I question my own sanity in believing that alternate realities exist."

"Yet here you are," he countered.

"This is too chaotic." She shook her head even as she leaned closer to him. "There is too much going on. I keep expecting a doctor to wake me from a dream. That is the only explanation for how I feel for you, for how I've fallen..."

"Fallen?" he prompted.

"Fallen...into your...bed so easily," she finished weakly.

"Fallen in love with me," he corrected. "Say it. Say you love me. Admit it. I know what I feel can't just be one sided. You love me. I know you do."

"Gerard." Again she shook her head in denial. A small part of him twinged in agony at the gesture, but he didn't give up hope.

"If you really think this is a dream then what is the harm in admitting the truth?" He cupped her face with both hands, drawing her mouth close to his. Against her lips, he whispered, "I love you, Cecilia."

"This can't work," she protested.

"I love you."

"It's illogical and chaotic."

"I love you."

"It makes no sense. It can't go anywhere."

"I love you," he shouted enthusiastically.

Her eyes shut. "I love you, too, Gerard. It makes no sense, but I love you too."

He closed the distance between them, kissing her with all the passion in his heart. Nothing else mattered. The future was uncertain. He didn't know how they would make it work. All he knew was that he loved her, wanted her, needed her. For the rest of his life he would never regret any of it. Cecilia completed him. She was what he'd been searching for his whole life.

He wanted to tell her as much, but her kiss kept his lips against hers. The taste of her brushed over his tongue. Hands roamed over his body, pulling at his clothes. He let her undress him, eager to explore her yet again. No matter how often he held her, he would never tire of making love to his woman.

Mine.

The reality of her filled his heart. He knew he'd

forced her to say the words, but she meant them. He saw the love in her expression even as she tried to fight it.

"This is chaos," she said against his mouth, still kissing him.

Gerard pulled back to study her face. Her lids fell heavy over her eyes, as if she was entranced. Her moist lips parted as she gasped for breath. For a moment, he couldn't move. She was so beautiful. The texture of her full lips captured his notice. He reached to run a finger over the bottom length. They were warm from the kiss.

Her fingers tapped along his arms. The scent of nature surrounded them. He loved the outdoors, but not as much as he loved her. Heat filled him, centering in his loins. Every part of him focused on her. Before he realized what he was doing, he had her stripped of her clothing.

When she was naked, standing before him, he took a step back. He quickly rid himself of his remaining clothing. She smiled at him, letting him look at her. Spots of sunlight came through the trees. The sterile suits and clothes littered the forest floor. A breeze whipped over them, rustling the leaves and chilling the skin. She shivered, her nipples budding.

His cock tightened and he shifted his weight.

Lifting his hand, he beckoned her to him. She came willingly. Their fingers threaded together as he led her deeper into the trees to a patch of softer grass. His desire for her only increased.

He kneeled on the grass, taking her with him. When he lay on his back so she could straddle his waist, she came over him with sunlight dancing around her. He liked this position. It freed his hands to roam the length of her body. Soft skin and supple flesh pressed to his.

Cecilia ran her hands over his chest to his neck. She cupped his face tenderly as her body lifted to take his cock inside. They came together, making love in the gently sanctuary of the forest. Gerard could never remember being so happy.

Cecilia tensed, her pussy tightening along his shaft. He answered the call of her body, finding his release in unison with hers. Afterwards she lay on his chest. Her breath tickled his neck. Gerard became aware of a rock digging into his ass but he didn't dare move and break the tranquility of the moment.

"You're limping." Sam frowned, eyeing Gerard.

"It's nothing. I'll take care of it." Gerard resisted the urge to rub his bruised ass. He'd managed to hide the injury from Cecilia when they walked inside. He'd thought he was alone when Dr. Swift joined him from a side office.

Sam automatically started leading Gerard to an exam room. When they were alone, he motioned Gerard to pull down his pants. "I spoke with Dr. Lu. He had a meeting with Dimensional Plane 303's politicians. They are not happy with the change in plans and threatened to inform Divinity Corporation if their dignitaries are not returned on schedule. The Medical Supreme neglected to inform us of an Anti-Chaos treaty he signed with them. We have no choice. Health risk or not, we have to send the women back in two weeks."

"Two?" Gerard stiffened. His heart beat hard. Just moments before he'd had an indefinite amount of time. "They were not scheduled to originally leave for almost four weeks."

"Apparently the fact we even requested an extension for their dignitaries has given 303's Politician Shinclus the idea that he has negotiating power. He has started making demands."

"Negotiation power? Why? Because we want to give them more information? You figure he'd be grateful."

"The Medical Supreme authorized some personal trades so he thinks he can make demands."

Gerard frowned, thinking of all the artifacts the Medical Supreme had in his home. He'd admired them on many occasions. "Politician Shinclus thinks he has power over us based on a few cultural artifacts the Medical Supreme wants to decorate his home with?"

"I don't understand the politician's reasoning. It must be a 303 cultural trait. Dr. Lu is handling the situation, but it's been decided to end their stay as soon as possible." Sam reached to the medical panel and filled a syringe. He jabbed it in the middle of

Gerard's sore muscle. The bruise began to heal as the medicine repaired the muscle tissue beneath it. Sam continued, "It is the only power play we have to show 303 we're in control."

"Surely the Medical Supreme will not allow…" Gerard pulled up his pants and turned to face Sam.

"The Medical Supreme is the one who ordered it. Lu convinced him to give us two weeks. He reluctantly agreed." Sam didn't look happy about the news. Why would he? They locked down the portal for a reason.

"We need more time. What if it spreads?" Gerard shook his head. "We can't risk infecting another plane."

"The Medical Supreme has spoken."

"He's sick." Gerard lowered his voice. "He may not be in the best position to make that decision."

Sam held up his hand, stopping Gerard from saying more. Already the words bordered on treason. "We have no medical proof of that."

"Sam, please." Gerard's eyes fell. He took a deep breath. "I can't send her back. Not yet. Don't ask me to."

"I suspected there may be more to you two when I saw the dirt on your back." Sam gave a long sigh. "Are you petitioning to have her stay as your wife?"

Gerard hadn't thought of that. "She doesn't want to stay. She is very attached to her home. As much as I care for her, I can't force her to stay with me. She may come to resent me if I did. I need more time to convince her to love this place or to find a way to go with her."

"You know the Medical Supreme would never agree to letting you go. With your knowledge, it would be seen as a medical database walking through the portal." Sam went to the monitor and scrolled through Gerard's medical readings. "You really do love her."

"I don't need the monitor to tell me that." Gerard gave a soft chuckle, but he wasn't really amused.

"I did," Sam answered. "We have two weeks. I feel for your plight, but our first order of business will be to find out how this disease is spread and how it mutates. If we can prove that it's contagious we can override the Medical Supreme's order and keep them here."

As much as Gerard wanted more time with Cecilia, he couldn't wish their mystery illness to be highly contagious. He loved her, but he didn't want her harmed. A war waged inside him, selfish desires against moral duty. Duty won. It had to. "And if not, at least then I will know she's safe."

17

CECILIA WASN'T sure what to think. She stood alone in her room, feeling as if her body were spinning in circles even as she remained still. Nothing made sense. A lifetime of anti-chaos warned her against falling in love with a man who didn't exist on her plane of reality. But it was too late. She had. She'd fallen in love with Gerard.

Her logical mind tried to analyze the situation, desperately wanting to reason how it happened. He was kind; she saw that in how he talked to others. He was smart. He made her laugh and smile, and somehow convinced her to break the law of her host plane and make love in the forest. He made her heart beat faster and her head forget everything she'd ever known to be true. He was chaos and she loved it, loved him.

She hadn't meant for any of it to happen. Cecilia was keenly aware of the job she was sent to do. In that she was failing. The pressure of it dampened her mood. She doubted the politicians would accept, "My apologies, I didn't manage to bring anything of real value back from a medically advanced plane, but I had some great sex and fell in love. Thank you for trusting me to take the trip. It was fun."

Then there was the little fact that she might not be going home any time soon. The idea of it didn't terrify her as it had before, but she knew she didn't want to live in the world that was so narrowly focused. She missed her mandatory grooming appointments and non-work days having breakfast with friends in the trollypark. She missed workout wheels, watching panel debates, clothes without layers, and the smell of non-sanitized air. And she most definitely missed not having to listen to an irritating wall monitor ding, forcing her to take yet another shot in her neck.

With a low growl, she went to the wall and took the syringe. Not bothering to look at the doses, she stuck it in her neck and recycled the injector. She did not want to do that for the rest of her life.

Cecilia knew she should go to her laboratory and get to work, but she couldn't force herself to leave the room. What did it matter? She was trapped on this plane until they developed a cure. It wasn't as if she understood half of what she read of their records anyway. For a smart woman, with an intelligence level to be proud of on her world, she felt completely useless and stupid on this one.

"At least I have time to figure this out," she told herself.

18

"WHAT DO YOU MEAN TWO WEEKS?" Cecilia was very aware she'd spent most of the day cursing the fact she was going to be trapped on a different level of reality. She had tried to focus on reading the files she'd been given access too, but her mind had wandered. Linnea was nowhere to be found, and Cecilia was actually glad for it. Now, as Gerard told her she was going home early, she wasn't ready to leave. "We were scheduled for four more."

"I thought you would be pleased. With the threat..." He didn't come to her, barely looked at her.

She searched his face, trying to bring froth the man she'd made love to in the forest. "I'm confused. One moment it's not safe to go. The next moment we have two weeks."

Gerard tensed, as if he didn't know what to say.

"You are right. My going is logical." Her brain agreed, but her heart didn't feel the same. "I should be grateful. What changed?"

"One of your politicians tried to renegotiate the terms of your agreement when we offered to extend your visit."

"Shinclus," Cecilia concluded, frowning. The man had a lot of power and even more lack of tactfulness.

"With our plane's current situation and the political climate between our worlds, it was deemed best that we send you home with the hope of trying again in the future."

"The future," she repeated. "So after two weeks, I may never see you again." Cecilia didn't bother to hide the tears entering her eyes. Her nose burned with the desire to cry. She closed the distance between them. "What if I want to stay the four?"

"You want to stay now?" He finally met her eyes.

"No. Yes. No." She lifted her arms helplessly. "I don't know. I miss my home. I miss my friends. I miss the food and the music. I miss color. Everyone here dresses the same and has the same hair and same smell."

His eyes softened.

"But you're here," she whispered. "If you could come with me..."

"That's not possible. No medical database is allowed to leave here. With what I know, it would never be allowed." He pulled her closer. "We'll figure something out."

"It's not like we can send communications to each other or visit each other on work breaks." She pushed weakly at his chest. "I told you from the beginning this couldn't go anywhere, that it couldn't mean anything. There will be this invisible wall between us, keeping us apart. We will spend our entire lives waiting on the whims of our politicians that I can someday come back."

"You would wait?"

"What do you think love is?" Cecilia responded, her voice rising. "You think I'll just go home through the portal and it will all go away?"

"Doctor."

Cecilia stiffened, startled by Linnea's intrusion. "What!" she answered, a little too harshly.

Linnea's face hardened. She stood in the doorway.

"What is it?" Cecilia said, softer, trying to amend her tone.

"Dr. Swift sent me to inform you we're leaving

the facility in the morning." Linnea's voice was flat and emotionless.

"I didn't mean to yell at you." Cecilia looked helplessly at the woman then Gerard. "I'm overwhelmed at the moment."

Linnea appeared cautious, but her expression did lighten. "I understand." She nodded once and left them alone.

"Cecilia." Gerard pulled her into his arms. The tight muscles of his chest pressed into her. She shivered, taking in his comfort. She didn't want to leave him. "I love you. I don't have answers for the rest, but I love you."

I love you. There was nothing more to say beyond that. Words would not change their reality.

"Spend the night with me," she said, forgetting all about trying to find something useful for her plane. "You'll leave with me tomorrow, won't you?"

"Of course. I'll stay with you every second I can."

Cecilia took his hand, not caring who saw them as she led him out of the laboratory into the hall. Her steps quickened. She pulled him into her room not wanting to waste a single moment. Barely waiting for the door to close, she kissed him. She poured everything she had into that kiss, holding nothing back.

Passion always simmered beneath the surface,

and now it raged between them. A feeling of desperation and sadness filled her. She tried to grab on to the moment, but felt it slipping past. Soon they were naked and his hands were on her body, urging her to her back. They made love slowly, savoring what they could.

As they climaxed in unison, his cock deep inside her, she whispered, "I love you, Gerard." What else could she say?

THE TRANSPORT STOPPED before Central Hospital. Cecilia lifted her head from Gerard's shoulder. For the majority of the transport ride they'd worked on compiling the research of each individual scientist on the virus. Even though all the records simply referred to the patient as Infected Subject One, Cecilia knew it was the Medical Supreme. Subject Two and Subject Three were part of his medical staff who had been working closely with him.

Cecilia didn't readily move to get out. "I don't think I can help you with any of this. You have some of the best medical minds on any plane of existence. I feel stupid compared to your doctors."

"I don't know why you say that. You comprehend much more than most dignitaries who visit." He kissed her cheek. "Our system is not the fairest. You come, are given very little information and training, and then are sent home. Very few planes have left after one short dignitary mission with anything valuable. What you've done has set the tone for future dealings. That makes your time here a success."

"On my plane I can read something and I instantly understand it and can apply it practically. Here, I feel like someone handed me cave markings." She closed her eyes briefly as he kissed her cheek again. The transport door slid open, as if the unit wanted them out so it could go along its way.

"We have to hurry." Sam appeared at their open door.

"Hurry?" Gerard repeated, surprised.

"Dr. Lu informed me unofficially that the Medical Supreme has changed his mind. He's not letting them go home." Sam gestured for Cecilia's hand to help her down. "We must hurry and get you home before I receive the order and the portal room is sealed shut indefinitely."

"Changed his mind? Again?" Gerard shook his head. "But..."

"There is no time." Sam practically pulled Cecilia from the transport. She stumbled. Gerard was right behind her, grabbing hold of her arm to steady her. As they walked, Sam continued, "It appears airborne. If the Supreme's staff is infected, the incubation period is short. We would see more cases outside of quarantine. Now is the only chance you have. Once that order comes through—"

"What about Linnea?"

"She wanted to finish up some logs at the biosphacility and asked that we go ahead. She took a later transport and will be along in a couple hours. It's just you. You can't wait for her. You have to go now." Sam glanced at Gerard, giving him a strange look she didn't understand. He didn't give her much time to think but her first instinct was to protest. Two weeks was bad enough, but now it looked as if she had two minutes. She stopped walking. Sam continued on, talking as if they followed him.

"Gerard..." She shook her head. "This can't—"

"Gerard," Sam insisted.

Gerard leaned closer to her, lowering his voice. "This is your chance. If you go now, you can go home. Who knows when you'll have another opportunity? Things are uncertain here. I don't want your health at risk. If you go now, I'll know you're safe."

"What if I never see you again? They keep taking time away from us. How can the Medical Supreme do this? He can't keep changing his mind." She needed time to think and logic and decide. How could she when they were pushing her through the portal?

A beep sounded.

"The official notice," Sam said, looking at the monitor. "They know we're here. I can't wait too long to read it."

"I can't ask you to stay," Gerard said to her, almost desperate. "I know how important your world is to you. This world is not safe, not right now."

She felt as if her heart was breaking. "Come with me."

"I need special permission." Gerard looked helplessly at Sam. She didn't care if the other doctor listened.

"Come anyway." Her heart beat faster. "I don't care about the anti-chaos laws. I'll deal with my politicians."

"There is no more time." Sam reached into his lab coat pocket and pulled out a syringe. "This will boost your immune system just in case, but it will also make you tired." He jabbed it in her arm before she could protest. "You must go now. For the sake of both our planes. Your world will be upset if we keep their doctor."

"But, Lin—" Cecilia swayed as the medicine

fogged her mind, unable to voice her concern over Linnea.

"I'll take care of her. I promise." Then to Gerard, he said, "You can't go, no matter how you want to. You don't have permission and your plane needs you here. The virus..."

Sam kept talking, but Cecilia didn't hear the rest. The man made sense, but she wanted to find something to say to protest the words. Her head swam with the shot he'd given her and the rush of emotion churning inside her body.

Family, life, world or Gerard?

Cecilia opened her mouth to say she wanted to stay but no words came out. She again swayed on her feet.

"The medicine might be strong. Linnea mentioned how much the inter-dimensional travel hurt their particular biology. This will make it easier on her. Help her," Sam insisted. "Go."

Gerard took her arm and rushed her toward the portal door. Her feet stumbled but she managed to stay upright. Everything was happening too fast.

Sam stayed back. When she looked down the hall, she saw the man answering the monitor summons.

Gerard walked her into the portal room. He

pulled her into his arms and kissed her hard. "I thought we'd have more time."

"Ask me to stay," she whispered. Her head swam. The words were slurred.

"I can't do that. I know how much your home means to you." He went to a control panel and began pushing buttons.

"Ask anyway." She felt her lips move, but she didn't hear the words. Her vision became very narrow and focused. She stared at Gerard, not wanting to leave him. She willed him to understand her thoughts, as she tried to hold on to them.

"I promise. As soon as I can, I will petition to have you brought back here. I love you, Cecilia. I will never forget you. I will wait." Gerard kissed her with a sense of urgency. She could tell by his body's response he wanted to do more, but they were out of time. He walked her to the platform. Her legs weakened and she sat on the floor. He let her go. She tried to grab on to him. Gerard pried her hands from his wrist and stepped back toward the door. "There is so much I want to say to you. I'll wait forever."

Cecilia reached for him but couldn't move. Tears came down her face. "Please," she mouthed.

They were out of time. Four weeks became two became none, all within the course of a day. She felt her heart breaking. That combined with the medicine made her incapable of speaking or moving. She begged him with her eyes to make time stop. There had to be a way.

He reached his hand behind him for the door. If she had known she was leaving, she would have said more in the transport. The blue light became brighter. The moment before it blinded her, she saw Sam join Gerard through the crack in the door. The burning in her flesh as she was ripped through the portal was nothing compared to the pain in her chest. Whatever Sam had given her helped the bone-shattering, muscle-disintegrating pain of portal travel, but it left her limp.

The portal tore her apart and put her back together. She fell to her stomach and didn't try to move. Her head swam, part from stunned grief, part from the shot she'd been given. The cool floor pressed to her cheek and a hot tear slipped over her face.

"Identify yourself."

She drew her head up to look at the control booth. Cecilia took several deep breaths. This was her world, but it felt surreal. She weakly lifted her hand in the green light, trying to block its brightness.

"Dr. Markos?"

She didn't recognize the voice. Feet shuffled toward her as the light dimmed. She was surrounded by private orderkeepers. Someone grabbed her foot and pulled off her shoe. She heard her identification number being read and a voice confirming her identity.

"Get her up," someone ordered.

"What happened to you?" another asked.

"Why are you back?" She recognized Shinclus over a speaker.

It was one voice she was compelled by a lifetime of law-abiding to answer. "They sent me." It wasn't much of an answer, but it was all she could manage in her drugged state. Someone repeated her words louder.

"And the other one?" Shinclus asked.

Cecilia shook her head.

"Just as well. Linnea Nel is untraceable," Shinclus said, giving no more concern to Linnea. "Someone help Dr. Markos to her feet. Call the government groomer and get her presentable before anyone sees her and she makes the news for not being sanitary. She looks terrible. Make sure the groomer wears protective gear. Then get her into quarantine and have her health checked."

Gerard stared at the door, unable to move. His hand shook, and he pressed it against the metal. He imagined he could feel the exact second she was pulled through the portal to her home world.

"I'm sorry. There was no time." Sam put a hand on his shoulder. "The order came through. If I had waited, she wouldn't have been able to leave at all. You told me how important it was to you that you didn't force her to stay."

"I didn't get to say all I needed to." Gerard felt as if he were dying. How could he live on the hope of maybe seeing her again when losing her hurt so badly?

"You did what you had to." Sam sighed. "I'm under orders to lock down the portal. We should go."

Gerard started to answer but saw Linnea stumbling down the hall. "I thought you said Sans Nel missed the transport."

"I..." Sam tried to lie. Gerard saw it on his face. The man looked to the floor.

"You trapped her here. You made me give up Cecilia and you trapped Linnea?" Gerard balled his fists. Anger built in him and he struck out, pushing Sam in the chest. The man fell back into the wall and didn't fight back.

"What is...?" Linnea's voice was weak.

"I had to," Sam whispered.

"I love her!" Gerard yelled. "Look at me. We just sent the most vital part of who I am through that portal." He pointed at a nearby monitor to his readings. It dinged several times demanding he take a shot to calm himself. "Look!"

Sam glanced behind to Linnea as she stumbled closer. "Then go. Take your chances. Go. Follow her. Just go. I'll say you were sent as a dignitary. I'll say it was to maintain peace." Sam reached for the wall and grabbed a clipboard. He handed it to Gerard along with a medical unit from his lab coat. "These will help ease your way with the 303 politicians once you get there."

Gerard didn't think. His rage turned instantly to

excitement and fear. What if Cecilia didn't want him to follow her? What if her plane rejected him? Feared him? Locked him away? It didn't matter. He would risk any punishment for her.

"I'll take Linnea," Gerard said, making a move to help the woman.

Sam grabbed his arm and shook his head in denial. "No. That's the deal. She stays. She will be invaluable to helping stop this disease. Now go. They'll be watching to make sure this section is sealed. If I don't do it, they'll do it for me offsite."

"But..." Gerard frowned. He read the man's expression. Linnea would be safe. "Thank you."

"We'll meet again," Sam assured him. "As soon as this is all over I'll send word."

"Good luck." Gerard pushed through the door and into his future.

"You too."

CECILIA STARED at the quarantine wall, through the clear plastic, to the man at the other side. She'd given her accounting of what had happened. They only asked once about Linnea, seeming less concerned about the woman's fate than the lack of medical knowledge Cecilia brought back with her.

"It has been two weeks. Why are you keeping me in here?" She didn't bother to keep the commanding tone out of her voice.

Dr. Tregeo looked up from his paper and frowned. She hated looking at him directly. Though he looked nothing like Gerard, Tregeo's eyes were brown. Gerard had brown eyes. Beautiful, deep, soulful brown eyes. The memory of them hurt her deep inside. She missed him. At night she fought the urge to cry out for him.

"As I have explained before, you will be released when we are satisfied we know everything that happened," Tregeo said.

Cecilia refused to talk about Gerard. It was none of their concern and she wouldn't sully the memory of him by having them write his name in their records as her lover. Whenever a new mission came up, *if* it came up, that would keep her name off the return list.

"I don't know what else I can tell you. The food was bland. They all wore the same color. The air smelled so sweet from sanitizer, it can be hard to breathe. They are dealing with an unknown virus of unknown origin. It is quarantined, but they ended all missions until further notice. The Medical Supreme is a very cautious man. I only met him once, but he—"

"You have told us all that," Tregeo interrupted. "Numerous times."

"Then what else do you want?" Cecilia leapt to her feet and yelled.

Tregeo jumped at the chaotic display and dropped his papers. She saw he'd been drawing a very poor likeness of her and not taking notes.

"What is going on?" she demanded.

Tregeo rushed away from her, hurrying down the corridor. Cecilia gave a small laugh. She pressed her head to the plastic and watched him disappear from her line of sight.

"You're a very lucky lady."

Cecilia opened her eyes to look at Politician Shinclus standing opposite her quarantine wall.

"Lucky?" It wasn't the sarcastic comment she wanted to make. She wanted to reference her fine accommodations and offer to trade places with him.

"Tregeo insisted you be brought up on anti-chaos charges for your little display." Shinclus waited, as if watching for some terrified reaction. She merely stood, watching him in return. "I intervened on your behalf, though the man had every right to charge you. I assured him that your outburst toward him would not happen again, but he has been transferred for his safety out of your presence."

Had her plane always been so overly dramatic?

She frowned. Then, belatedly, she nodded at Shinclus and mumbled, "Many thanks."

Shinclus smiled, the kind of benevolently irritating look people got when they thought themselves powerful and bestowing. "If you assure me you can behave yourself, I'll let you out of there."

"Tregeo is dramatic," Cecilia said very calmly. "Did you see the papers he left on the floor?"

"I did. They don't look like you at all. Your endowments are smaller." Shinclus lifted his hand to give the command she be released.

The sliding door brought with it a rush of cool air. She took a deep breath. "Has there been any word from Plane 187?"

"Not since your arrival," he answered.

"Linnea Nel? Should we attempt to make contact to get her back? I can go since I know everyone." She kept the hope out of her voice.

"I think it's for the best they keep her. She can't be scanned, you know." He didn't meet her eyes as he walked faster.

"She was an asset," Cecilia insisted. "We can't leave her there."

"It has been handled." He refused to look at her.

"Wait, that's why no one asked me about her?

You made arrangements that they should keep her." Cecilia stopped in disbelief.

"The Medical Supreme agreed that he would find a place for her in his home," Shinclus said. "It's more than someone like her could hope for. I daresay the crime rate will drop by fifty-five percent now that she is gone. Do you know how many times she was caught reading in the library? Medical texts even. She is not authorized to study medicine. An untraceable woman cannot be given such knowledge. Who knows what she would do with it. Order must be maintained, and with her permanently off plane it has been."

The fact the elections were coming up and Politician Shinclus would personally take credit for the fall in crime probably had a lot to do with it.

"Don't look so stricken," Shinclus scolded. "She knows all about it. She was ordered not to tell you and distract from your mission. She'll be much happier there. She wants to read medical texts, and there she can."

The man's words made sense, though she didn't trust him completely. Linnea had seemed fairly comfortable at the biosphacility and she hadn't come to Central Hospital with Dr. Swift.

"What I want to know is why you haven't told

us more about Dr. Fauchet." Shinclus paused at the end of the hall, waiting for someone to open the door for him. A guard grabbed the handle and pulled it open. She followed Shinclus into a small waiting area that would take her outside the facility.

Cecilia tried to remain calm. How could they know about her relationship with Gerard? Had she given something away? Cried out his name in her sleep? "What do you mean? I listed him as a contact in my reporting of events."

"You did." Shinclus didn't stop. He kept going, past the chairs to another secure door. A guard held it open when he saw them coming. Cecilia noticed the man eyed her as she passed, as if her crazy reputation with Dr. Tregeo preceded her. Why hadn't she noticed her plane's anti-chaos extremism before? No wonder Linnea wanted to leave.

As much as she'd wanted to come home, now it felt empty. She didn't belong on 187 but now she felt displaced on her own world. She looked at the people she passed. They had no idea what she had been through, what she had seen, what was really out there. She looked at the walls and imagined she could see Central Hospital's walls. It shifted from reality. Was Gerard standing where she was now? Unseen?

Untouchable? As much a ghost to her as she was to him?

"Dr. Markos?" Shinclus looked at her expectantly.

"Where are we going? I'm ready to go home. My family—"

"Your family does not expect you for another two weeks." The politician led the way into the secure hall, away from the waiting area, deeper into the facility. He went through several doors.

"There is nothing more I can do," she said, hesitant to follow him. It was possible they'd lock her in another cell.

"Nothing?" Shinclus asked. Then stopping, he frowned. "I understand now. Your psychological work-up did not have you marked for political shrewdness, but now I see we underestimated you. They wondered why you were withholding key information about your contacts, but I see how you want to negotiate. Well done, Dr. Markos. I see my choosing you for this mission was well done indeed. So, what do you want?"

"What do I want?" she repeated slowly, trying to figure out what he meant.

Shinclus gave a small, knowing smile. Cecilia had never been more confused. "I can offer top-level housing. The movers will pack your belongings and have you in the new south tower complex today."

"I—" Cecilia began, only to be cut off. South tower was very high end. People would spend a lifetime on a waiting list just to get in to a place like that.

"No, before you try to negotiate, hear the rest." Shinclus stopped walking. "This alliance is important to us. You more than anyone understand that. You'll get an executive office and laboratory at your disposal in the most secure facility. You will be provided with a key to the private tram."

The private tram? Only top-level government officials used the tram. It had spa services and fine dining and delivered its passengers to private decks at the most luxurious places in town.

"You are a hard negotiator," Shinclus said at her silence. "This of course will mean you receive more compensation, trip allowance, and your own staff."

"Thank you." Cecilia tried to sound assertive, but really she was more worried now than before. They thought she knew more than she did.

"This way." Shinclus seemed pleased with himself. "You begin work immediately."

"Immediately," Cecilia protested. "What exactly is it you expect me to do?"

"Your job." Shinclus motioned to a guard. The man stepped to the side.

Cecilia slowly walked into the room, not sure what to expect. Seeing a man with his back toward her, she first noticed his lab coat. It was 187 issued. Her breath caught. Her eyes flew up toward his head. It wasn't Gerard.

"Dr. Swift," she acknowledged, racked with disappointment.

"Dr. Markos." The man smiled. "I'm pleased to see you are well."

"Cecilia?"

Cecilia turned, gasping at the sound of Gerard's voice. He stood in the corner of the room. She made a weak noise. All thoughts left her. She rushed forward. She didn't care where she was, or who watched. Once she put her hands on him she was never letting go again.

"Gerard," she whispered, reaching for him. She wound her arms around his shoulders. The depths of his brown eyes caught hers and she knew she never wanted to look away. She kissed him, deep and passionate. She heard words around them but she ignored them. His hands found her hips, pulling her close. The last two weeks disappeared. Tears filled her eyes. When she leaned away from his mouth, one drop slid over her cheek. "How?"

"I understand now," Shinclus said behind her. "Well played, Dr. Markos."

Cecilia touched Gerard's face, ignoring Shinclus. "How?"

"Cecilia," Gerard whispered. He smiled at her and she felt her insides melt a little.

Sam cleared his throat. "Dr. Markos, I came with good news. Your proposal was accepted by the Medical Supreme. You made a fine argument."

Cecilia blinked, glancing over her shoulder. She pulled out of Gerard's arms but took up his hand and held it in both of hers.

"We are very grateful for your plane's hospitality. Dr. Fauchet's two-week quarantine, though inconvenient considering out stringent health guidelines before travel, is understandable. I came to check up on him just as soon as I could get away. I'm happy to hear he will be staying with you."

Two weeks? Gerard had followed her through the portal? Why hadn't anyone told her? She opened her mouth to respond, but there was a seriousness to Sam's words and expression, an insistence that she go along with what he was saying, so she stayed quiet.

"Yes," Gerard said quickly. "Completely under-standable."

Cecilia didn't speak, finding it best to try not to look too confused. It was then she noticed the streak of purple in Gerard's brown hair. He'd been groomed and he smelled of government-approved soap. Then she noticed his clothing—a one–piece, pale blue suit that looked very much like her quarantine garb.

"There are some formalities, naturally." Shinclus puffed out his chest. "An identification number will be assigned and a chip implanted immediately. We will also need you to file papers regarding your sexual relations status. 187's consent forms cannot be entered into public record, as 187 technically does not exist. I am assuming you filed all of the correct forms before initiating contact?"

"Of course," Gerard said mimicking Shinclus's serious tone. "Dr. Markos is very thorough with her paperwork. It is my intention to conform to all 303 laws and regulations."

"Dr. Markos will be your liaison." Shinclus gave a small laugh. "I assume that is agreeable. As long as you abide by all our anti-chaos laws there will be no issue. Will you require your own home?"

"He'll stay with me," Cecilia said finding her voice.

"Very good," Shinclus agreed, looking at Sam. "Dr. Markos will keep him from wandering into the wrong neighborhoods. Now that is settled, I will leave Dr. Markos to begin orientation. Dr. Swift, I believe you mentioned something about technology."

"Yes, but we have very strict guidelines as to how and who may use it. All devices will be biocoded to Dr. Markos and Dr. Fauchet." Sam glanced in her direction and gave a small smile before moving to follow Shinclus out of the room.

"Wait," Cecilia beckoned him. "Sans Nel? Is she...?"

"She is well. She has agreed to stay with us as part of the exchange program." Sam looked sideways at Shinclus. "As you proposed."

Cecilia nodded. When Shinclus turned his back, Sam mouthed, "She is well taken care of."

"Thank you, Dr. Swift," Cecilia held Gerard's hand tighter.

"Until we meet again, Dr. Markos." Sam left, closing the door behind him.

When they were alone, Cecilia pulled Gerard closer. "What is going on? Is the virus cured? When did you get here? How did you come through the portal? They were closing it down. I saw you disappear when I was pulled through. How did you manage to convince the Medical Supreme to let you come? I thought he would never agree to it. I thought I would never see you again. How is this possible? Is the Medical Supreme dead? Is that why you are allowed to be here? And is Linnea really all right with the trade? I didn't get a chance to talk to her. Though, I'm not giving you back. They can't take you. They won't try to take you back, will they? How long can you stay?"

Gerard's smile only widened until finally he cut off her rush of words with a quick kiss and a laugh. "Are you nervous? Is that why you are speaking so fast?"

"You said the same thing to me in the transport my first day on your plane." Her body heated at the memory. They had made love for the first time on the trip. It felt so long ago. So much had changed.

"I remember. You were so flustered."

"How are you here, Gerard?" She stroked his face and neck before touching the colored streak in his hair.

"Do you like it?" he asked, clearly excited. "I couldn't decide which kind to get, so I let the groomer choose. Did you know that I could have my whole head green?"

Cecilia nodded. "Yes, I did know that."

"Of course you did."

"Gerard? My questions? How much time do we have?"

"Only forever," he answered. "I am 303's new permanent liaison, thanks to Sans Nel's excellent work on 187. She is very well, by the way. You have no need to worry about her. The Medical Supreme is alive. The virus is under control. I came through about two seconds after you did. They wouldn't tell me where you were and I refused to talk to anyone but you. Strange though, they wanted to groom me before a health check. We should probably work on getting that protocol changed. Then Sam showed up with a trade agreement two days ago. Aside from the required trips back, I'm now a member of New Order Society."

"Only forever?" she repeated. Her heart beat fast. "I don't know if that is enough time."

"We better not waste it then." He playfully brushed his nose against hers. "I remember the first day you came to my plane. You couldn't keep your hands off me and I knew that first second I wanted to be with you."

"You kissed me," she protested, trying not to laugh. "It was very presumptuous of you, Dr. Fauchet."

"You kissed me back, Dr. Markos."

"Mm." She lifted up on her toes and let her mouth move against his. "Yes, I did. I will always kiss you back, Gerard. I love you. Only forever."

"Only forever, my love." His lips met hers in passion.

The End

Linnea's Arrangement
(Divinity Healers 3)
by Michelle M. Pillow

Beautiful, highly intelligent Linnea Nel wants what most women want—a career, love, respect. But coming from a plane where order and all things anti-chaos reign, the untrackable, untraceable and highly rebellious Linnea is considered a threat—to her family, society and her world. When her numerous arrests for reading library books become a public embarrassment to her politically minded sister, Linnea is forced on a dignitary mission to an alternate reality.

There are only two classifications of people on

plane 187: Doctors and Not Doctors (Sans). Dr. Sam Swift is one of the highest ranking officials on the medical plane, answering only to the Medical Supreme. When the Medical Supreme becomes ill, it's up to him to find a cure. Nowhere in this equation is there room—or time—to fall in love. And then he meets the exquisitely frustrating Sans Linnea Nel.

In the midst of the worst outbreak 187's society has faced in decades, two people who never should have met fall in love. How can Linnea stay where she may be in danger? But how can Sam let the love of his life go?

For more information, visit www.Michelle-Pillow.com

Chapter One Excerpt

New Order Society, Dimensional Plane 303

Linnea Nel eyed the bars of her cell. The New Order Society government wouldn't keep her locked up long. They never did. For every second she stayed in jail, the higher her offender ranking number would go. Since all number statistics were reported to the public, they would prefer she was ranked as a misdemeanor disturbance as opposed to anything major—like thievery or, worse, public chaos.

As one of the few people whose body's natural magnetism didn't allow for the anti-chaos implant, she was on every government and societal watch list. As a child, she'd managed to blend. Linnea had been a good student, a model participant in societal functions. Then came graduation. No higher learning institutes would take her. They didn't even bother to give her a good reason why she was rejected. Without an implant, they had no way of ensuring she did her own coursework and followed institutional policies. So it didn't matter how good she was or how smart. Unlike all other students, she would never be under their complete monitoring and control. They couldn't risk putting her into a position of power. They couldn't risk educating her. So she'd educated herself.

"Come on out of there, Nel," Orderkeeper Delkin said. The man should have instilled fear in her with his Goliath size, but Linnea had been in his cell way too many times. "And don't let us catch you in the library again without permission."

"Wouldn't dream of it," she answered dryly.

"Yeah," he muttered. "You know what to do.

When you're checked out of the system, there's some people here waiting to talk to you."

People? Linnea frowned. Her own parents barely spoke to her—the uncontrollable one. Since she moved into New Order City, they hadn't really spoken to her. Why should they when her older brother and sister both did the family proud? Her genetic fluke only caused them embarrassment. To society's way of thinking, since she couldn't be watched, she was destined to cause trouble. She'd stopped trying to impress her parents years ago. Some battles couldn't be won, so there was no point in fighting them.

"See you next time around, keeper." Linnea typed in her identification number and made her way toward the front of the Orderkeeper Station. The tracking monitors made a familiar beep as she was scanned and found without a chip. They had tried making her wear a few around her neck, but her body's natural energy made them glitch. Once the monitor even read her as the wrong person—a dead singer, to be precise. That little event had raised a lot of alarms. There were still rumors that Silev had faked his own death and was really alive. What could she say? Diehard fans would believe anything. The only reason the orderkeepers didn't lock her up was because the authorities were fearful word of her condition would get out. Societal control depended on society trusting the implants implicitly.

"Linnea."

Linnea paused by the open door and slowly moved to stand in the doorway. Out of all the people who'd come to the station to get her, she never expected to see her sister. When they were little, Jinna had been her best friend. Now, looking at the woman, she couldn't see that little girl. Instead, she saw the pristine and orderly countenance of Politician Nel, new leader of the anti-chaotic task force.

"Jin," Linnea answered. Like everyone else on the planet, her sister wore the one-piece suit. Material that belled around the legs led to tightly-fitted hips and a looser bodice. Her black hair had been streaked along the side with a bright, unnatural red, and tiny jewels had been adhered in a swirl pattern along the inside of it.

Linnea preferred to keep her black hair shorter with a streak of dark purple to match the purplish grey of her eyes. Her bodice was tight, less conservative in design. A thick, black belt wrapped her ribs, dark purple over black material.

"Leave us," Jinna ordered her two guards.

Linnea didn't back away as they passed, even as they stared at her like she was about to attack her own sister.

When they were alone, Linnea stepped into the room.

"This needs to stop," Jinna said. "I can't have a sister who's constantly being arrested for petty chaotic crimes."

"I'm great, thanks for asking, Jin," Linnea answered, moving to the long bench next to the wall. She took a seat and stretched her feet forward in easy repose. Smiling pleasantly, though she hardly felt pleasant, she inquired, "And you?"

"Always a child." Jinna frowned.

"Ah, Jin, I think you're being too hard on your-self. You've done well. I wouldn't call you a child." Linnea smirked. The look was a mask, a way of keeping the true depths of her hurt to herself. She wanted so badly to live a normal life, to have a family, find love and marry, have a career and a well-earned respect. Instead, she was arrested for daring to better herself.

"I didn't mean me," Jinna answered, flustered. "You are always a child. This proves my point. Do you ever think of anyone but yourself?"

Dropping all pretenses, Linnea drew her feet in

and placed her elbows on her knees. "I was reading a book, not running naked through the streets."

"Not this time," Jinna grumbled.

"Once. I ran naked through the streets once. I was angry. You would be too if your application to medical learning was denied because of a stupid inability to take an implant. My grades were better than yours. I passed all my tests. I had recommendations and—"

"I'm not here to debate the past," Jinna interrupted.

"It's not the past," Linnea said. "It's my present, my future." She leaned over, jerking off her boot to expose her bare foot. A black numbered tattoo stared back at them, her identification number. Normally, the implants would be placed underneath the visible mark. Those numbers were everything—her money access, her education and work history, her purchasing rations, her identification. Everyone living in the New Order Society had a designation. When they were children, the government trucks had visited their school. The technicians wore costumes as to not frighten them. They danced and sang as the coded implants were injected beneath every child's number. Linnea's body rejected the implant, and every one after that.

Her scarred foot attested to it. "It's not like I'm unwilling to be part of the system. I almost lost my foot to infection because I had the damned chip implanted too many times. I know the law. I know that this is the only way society can thrive. There must be order to chaos. You all just won't let me be a part of your society! It's not like I can help some natural electrical magnetism in my body—a current your doctors can't even define. Maybe if you let me go to school I could figure it out. I could design a better implant."

"Funding will not be granted to cure one person, Linnea. The needs of the many will be met first."

"The needs of the many? Like using chemists to make better-smelling grooming products?" Linnea wanted to scream, but knew that would do no good. "I could do that too."

"I'm here to discuss your future." When Jinna looked at her, Linnea didn't feel as if her sister actually saw her.

"You're letting me go to school?" Hope filled her.

"You know I can't do that."

The hope died. Though she should have been used to it by now, the disappointment physically hurt. "Then what?"

"I've secured a position for you with Dr. Cecilia

Markos as an assistant." Jinna smiled for the first time.

"Assistant?"

"Don't look so disappointed. You clearly want to be in the medical field since you're constantly sneaking into the library to read medical textbooks."

"I read fiction too," Linnea said, just to be contrary. "Perhaps I really dream of being make-believe."

Even as part of her wanted to jump at the chance to be near medicine, another part knew that to be merely an assistant would eventually wear her down. To be so close and not be able to succeed. It would be torture.

"Dr. Cecilia Markos is fast becoming one of our greatest assets. You're lucky she's willing to take you with her."

"With her?" Linnea stood. "Where? Are you banishing me? New Order City is my home."

"Dr. Markos has been assigned to the off-plane program. You will be joining her on a trip through what we call the Divinity portal to a medically advanced dimensional plane in a parallel universe. It's primarily an ambassadorial journey, a basic trading of goodwill while gauging the plane's medical knowledge and their usefulness to our world."

"Portal travel?" Linnea felt a shiver work over her body. "I was joking when I said I wanted to be make-believe."

"When have you ever known me to joke?" Jinna arched a brow.

Good point.

"What do you mean a portal to a parallel universe?" she asked.

"Exactly that. You're smart, so I know I don't have to explain the concept of alternate realities and parallel universes to you. So take the theories you know and suppose they are real. Suppose someone found a way to move between the veils, so to speak. Looking at an alternate reality is like seeing our world if history had been altered in some way. Languages are similar, so you will not have a problem in that department. I'm told some people will look the same, but do not mistake them for being the same people. Humans will look like humans, save a few minor differences."

Linnea opened her mouth to speak, but said nothing. Jinna was serious.

"An entity called Divinity Corporation mastered the science of inter-dimensional travel. About two years ago they made contact with us. Since then, we've allowed a portal gate to be placed on our world.

We're one of four-hundred-thirty-six charted universes, with infinitely more out there. We plan on staking a big claim in Divinity's project. Several ambassadors have been sent through and have come back successfully. Dr. Markos will lead the medical team. You will be her assistant."

Linnea frowned. "Team?"

"Well, a team of two. You and her."

"Why haven't I heard of this?"

"And cause societal panic? No. The public will not be made aware of these developments. There is no need to concern them. The government knows what is best for them."

"What if I say no? What if I tell? Your secret would be out."

Jinna laughed. "Do you still believe you can make people listen to you? Lin, Lin, Lin." Jinna shook her head in amusement. "You don't have a choice. You're going. It's what is best for societal harmony. I'm sure you understand."

"And when it's over? When I come back?" Linnea stiffened, a strange feeling of dread unfurling inside her. But, this was her sister. She didn't want to believe that Jinna would do something to hurt her.

"Why don't you concentrate your efforts on dealing with today? My guards have the information you need." Jinna left, leaving Linnea to stare after her. No matter how fantastic her sister's words were, Linnea found the idea of an alternate reality easier to believe than Jinna actually teasing her with this ridiculous conversation.

New York Times & USA TODAY
Bestselling Author

Michelle loves to travel and try new things, whether it's a paranormal investigation of an old Vaudeville Theatre or climbing Mayan temples in Belize. She believes life is an adventure fueled by copious amounts of coffee.

Newly relocated to the American South, Michelle is involved in various film and documentary projects with her talented director husband. She is mom to a fantastic artist. And she's managed by a dog and cat who make sure she's meeting her deadlines.

For the most part she can be found wearing pajama pants and working in her office. There may or may not be dancing. It's all part of the creative process.

**Come say hello! Michelle loves talking
with readers on social media!**

www.MichellePillow.com

facebook.com/AuthorMichellePillow

twitter.com/michellepillow

instagram.com/michellempillow

bookbub.com/authors/michelle-m-pillow

goodreads.com/Michelle_Pillow

amazon.com/author/michellepillow

youtube.com/michellepillow

pinterest.com/michellepillow

COMPLIMENTARY EXCERPTS

TRY BEFORE YOU BUY!

THE SAVAGE KING
BY MICHELLE M. PILLOW

Lords of the Var® Book One by Michelle M. Pillow

Bestselling Catshifter Romance Series

Cat-shifting King Kirill knows he must do his duty by his people. When his father unexpectedly dies, it's his destiny to take the throne and all of the responsibility that entails. What he hadn't prepared for is the troublesome prisoner that's now his to deal with.

Undercover Agent Ulyssa is no man's captive. Trapped in a primitive forest awaiting pickup, she's going to make the best out of a bad situation...which doesn't include falling for the seductions of a king.

About *Lords of the Var*® (Books 1-5)

You met their father, King Attor, in Dragon Lords Books 1-4, now meet the Var Princes!

The cat-shifter princes were raised to not believe in love, especially love for one woman, and they will do everything in their power to live up to their father's expectations. Oh, how the mighty will fall.

The Savage King Excerpt

Kirill watched the door to his bedroom open. He'd been sitting in the dark, trying to relieve the stress headache that had built behind his eyes for the last week. The pain started at the base of his skull and radiated up to his temples until he could hardly see straight.

A heavy responsibility had been thrust on his shoulders, a responsibility he really hadn't prepared himself for, the welfare of the Var people. King Attor had not left him in a good position. He'd rallied the people to the brink of war, convinced them that the Draig were their enemy, and even went so far as to attack the Draig royal family.

Kirill wanted to see peace in the land. However, he knew the facts didn't bode well for it. The Draig had a long list of grievances against King Attor and the Var kingdom.

Before his death, the king had ordered an attack on the four Draig princes, all of which ended horribly for the Var. The worst was when Prince Yusef was stabbed in the back, a most cowardly embarrassment for the Var guard who did it. If he hadn't been executed in the Draig prisons, he would've been ostracized from the Var community. Luckily, Prince Yusef survived or they'd already be at battle.

Attor had also arranged for the kidnapping of Yusef's new bride. The Draig Princess Olena had been rescued, or that too would've led to war. The old king had even tried to poison Princess Morrigan, the future Draig queen, on two separate occasions. She too lived. And those were only a few of the offenses Kirill knew about in the few weeks before King Attor's death. He could just imagine what he didn't know.

Kirill sighed, feeling very tired. He'd known since birth that the day would come when he'd be expected to step up and lead the Var as their new king. He just hadn't expected it to be for another hundred or so years. His father had been a hard man, whom he'd foolishly believed was invincible.

"Here kitty, kitty, kitty." His lovely houseguest's whisper drew his complete attention from his heavy thoughts.

Ulyssa bent over like she expected him to answer to the insulting call. He dropped his fingers from his temple into his lap, and a quizzical smile came to his lips. As he watched her, he wasn't sure if he was angered or amused by her words.

"Are you in here, you little furball?" she said, a little louder.

She wore his clothes. Never had the outfit looked sexier. His jaw tightened in masculine interest, as he unabashedly looked her over. All too well did he remember the softness of her body against his and the gentle, offering pleasure of her sweet lips. She'd made soft whimpering noises when he'd touched her, yielding, purring sounds in the back of her throat. Even with the aid of nef, he was surprised by how easily and confidently she melted into him. The Var were wild, passionate people and were drawn to the same qualities in others. He suspected she'd be an untamed lover.

Too bad she'd belonged to his father first. In his mind, that made her completely untouchable though none would dare question his claim if he were to take her to his bed. Technically, by Var law, she belonged to him until he chose to release her. For an insane moment, he thought about keeping her as a lover. He knew he wouldn't, but the thought was entertaining.

Kirill's grin deepened. Ulyssa strode across his home to the bathroom door with an irritated scowl. It was obvious she didn't see him in the darkened corner, watching her. He detected her engaging smell from across the room, the smell of a woman's desire. It stirred his blood, making his limbs heavy with arousal. And, for the first time since his father's death, his headache relieved itself.

"Hum, maybe I'm looking too high. I'm sure there has to be a little cat door here somewhere. Come here, little kitty. Where are you hiding?"

His slight smile fell at her words. It was easy to detect her mocking tone.

"Where's your little kitty door, huh?" Ulyssa whispered to herself, her blue gaze searching around in the dark.

Kirill grimaced in further displeasure. He watched her open the door to his weapons cabinet. Her eyes rounded, and he thought she might take one. She didn't. Instead, she nodded in appreciation before closing the door and continuing her search for an exit.

She stopped at a narrow window by his kitchen doorway. Her neck craned to the side, as she tried to see out over the distance. Kirill knew she looked at the forest. From under her breath, he heard her vehement whisper, "Where exactly did you little fur balls bring me? Ugh, I need to get out of this flea trap, even if I have to fight every one of you cowardly felines to do it. I've fought species twice as big and three times as frightening. A couple of little kitty cats don't scare me."

If this insolent woman wanted to play tough, oh, he'd play. Curling gracefully forward, Kirill shifted before his hands even touched the ground. He let one thick paw land silently on the floor, followed by a second. Short black fur rippled over his tanned flesh, blending him into the shadows. His clothes fell from his body, and he lowered his head as he crept forward. A low sound of warning started in the back of his throat. He was livid.

To find out more about Michelle's books visit www.MichellePillow.com

LILITH ENRAPTURED

BY MICHELLE M. PILLOW

Divinity Warriors Book One

Alternate Reality Romance

Sorin of Firewall lives in a land forever at war. In fact, the Starian men are so busy fighting, their marriage ceremony has been reduced to a "will of the gods" event where they simply pick a woman out of a lineup and claim her as a wife. With women becoming scarce, it's necessary to trade the offworld Divinity Corporation for brides. Duty-bound to attend the ceremony, he has no intention of picking a bride, let alone one from another dimension. That is, until he sees Lilith, the bewitching woman sent by the gods to reward—or punish?—him.

Lilith Enraptured Excerpt

Sorin took several deep breaths, feeling as he did when about to go into battle. Heat filled him as tension worked its way into his limbs. With a single thought, he could will his body to spring into action. He could erase her from the world and end this before it started.

But it was too late. He was lost the moment he'd looked at her, had seen her big blue eyes staring at him in trepidation. No, he was lost before that, when he felt her looking at him, beckoning him with her unwavering gaze to find her in the crowd.

Temptress. Witch.

He willed the desire inside him to go away. It shouldn't have been so strong. He'd relieved himself like he always did, had spilled his seed to ease the lonely ache.

Light from the fireplace shone through the white of her gown, silhouetting the long length of her legs and arms. The linen clung to her shoulders, swooping gently along the curves of her breasts— breasts that would be bare beneath. The tied hands were a new addition to the ceremony, thanks to Sir Aidan's wayward woman, Lady Paige. Sorin's barbaric side found he liked the addition.

Hunger rushed into every limb, lifting his cock beneath the long tunic. He didn't think to hide the reaction. No one would care. It had been so long, so very long, since he'd had a woman in his bed. He suppressed a groan. Soft flesh. Round breasts. Taut nipples. Slick, warm vessel to catch his passion. That certain female smell when he pressed his nose to her sex.

A thought whispered in the back of his mind. Maybe she's different. Maybe she'll be better. Maybe this one will stay.

He cursed the thought. No. She wasn't different. She wasn't better. Sorin had made up his mind long ago. He'd come, he'd look, but he never, ever wanted to find someone. He wasn't meant to have this, or her, or any kind of peace. Sorin was born into a land of war. He was made for it, every piece of him. One of the bloodiest battles in their history happened the very hour his mother gave birth to him.

Some were lucky to find peace in marriage, but not him. Tradition and necessity dictated he come to these ceremonies and try to find someone. He came from a noble line, a position of power, one that demanded he have sons to carry on his family's name. But society could not make him choose. It could not make him step forward and lay claim.

"Mine."

Where did that word come from? It sounded like his voice, booming over the hall to quiet all who watched into stunned silence. It felt like his body refusing to go to his place at the table, instead moving forward with arm uplifted to point at the blonde-haired beauty. But it couldn't be his body or his voice. That would mean he'd just announced his claim. Everyone would have heard it. He couldn't back out once the word was said.

"Sorin?" his younger brother, Ronen, hissed. Like Sorin, Ronen led one of the more renowned armies in all of Staria. Very few would dare to challenge their word or honor and the fact made it even more impossible for Sorin to take back what he'd done.

"Mine," Sorin found himself repeating. Was he possessed? What madness was this? He kept walking toward her. She merely stared at him, those wide, gorgeous eyes capturing his. Straight blonde hair hung long down her back, just as a woman's should.

"Brother?" Ronen questioned. The shock was evident in his voice. Sorin couldn't blame him for the surprise because that very day he'd been instructing Ronen to stay strong and not fall for a woman's pretty face. And what did Sorin do? He claimed a woman with a pretty face.

The hall remained quiet. Sorin stopped before the woman, noting with pleasure that she didn't cringe and fall away from his looming presence. Her strength would serve her well. Years of frustrated desires surged inside him. He couldn't put them off any longer. Deny it as he might, he needed a woman. He would never admit the words out loud. The need was not just for physical release, but for the softness of her, the sweet smell and the temporary relief from the endless fighting that such a creature could bring.

You tried this before, Sorin. Such things are not for you.

Fool.

Idiot.

Weak.

His accusing thoughts infuriated. Reaching for her bound arms, he took hold of the ropes. Not even his condescending inner voice could stop his actions. Sorin held her gaze steady, stating so she couldn't mistake his claim, "You are mine."

For a complete, up-to-date booklist, visit www.MichellePillow.com

www.ingramcontent.com/pod-product-compliance
Lightning Source LLC
Chambersburg PA
CBHW030631120726

47904CB00006B/2110